# Winter Passage

# Winter Passage

## Judith McDaniel

Spinsters, Ink
San Francisco

First Edition
10 - 9 - 8 - 7 - 6 - 5 - 4 - 3 - 2 - 1

Spinsters, Ink
803 De Haro St.
San Francisco, CA 94107

Cover Art: D. Worden
Cover Design: Linda Szyniszewski, Elephant Graphics
Text Design: Sherry Thomas
Typesetting: ComText Typography, Inc., San Francisco
Printed in the U.S.A.

Publication of this book was made possible in part through a loan from Holding Our Own, A Fund For Women.

ISBN: 0-933216-10-6

Library of Congress Catalog Card Number: 84-51049

*Individual contributions by 36 women helped to make possible the publication of this novel. Their support is gratefully acknowledged.*

# Chapter 1

## February, 1975

She watched the snow settling on the bare orchard branches. It would linger until a light wind scattered gauzy puffs back into the air leaving the dark twisted branches outlined against the slate sky. Many times Anna thought living in the orchard was like being inside a Japanese painting. The trees so pruned. So bare. Twisted. Each twig bore a fruit. Nothing extra allowed. This efficiency seemed at once unnatural and wonderful to her, a metaphor for the essentials of art, especially of poetry, that careful trimming back of words.

When the old horse let out her breath, Anna tightened the girth again on the saddle, then mounted quickly. The horse turned a reluctant head into the light snow and stepped carefully down the dirt road. Anna slouched western style in the slim English saddle. Her worn Oklahoma sheepherder's jacket and steel-toed work boots just didn't fit, she thought, as she two-handed the reins in best English style.

"Rose," she drawled, mocking the image she imagined others saw, "we're the odd couple. Couldn't you speak western instead of English on a day this cold? I'd like to keep a hand in my pocket." Rose's ears twitched back as Anna pressed her legs lightly to urge the horse into a faster walk down the long hill.

"Come down for Sunday brunch," Clair had said last week when they'd met in the co-op. "We're sugaring. In and out all day. I have to keep a dozen people warm and fed, so come on down."

"Thanks," Anna said, never meaning to go. She was too busy. There was too little time to be alone and Sunday was the best of those times.

But this morning she had sat at her typewriter and stared out of the window into the snow drifts piled around the little three room house. Then she turned to her desk and opened her journal, but her eyes returned to the snow and when she looked back at her journal, the page was dark after staring at the bright swirling snow. So she closed the journal and decided to ride Rose down the hill to the farm and see how the sugaring was going. If she rode the horse, her visit would seem more casual. Driving up in the car was too deliberate.

Clair opened the door to Anna's knock.

"Hi, I'm so glad to see you, I thought you'd be too busy to come, isn't it too cold to leave the horse out in the yard, can I have Tammie take her to the barn?"

Anna laughed at Clair's run on sentences. She shook the snow out of her hair and sat down to pull off her boots. "Don't worry about Rose. It's not that cold. I thought it had to be thawing or you couldn't sugar."

"I don't think it's running today. They're up at the barn boiling off yesterday's collection. Paul's a maniac when it gets to this point. He's too meticulous to be a farmer." She sat down at the table across from Anna. "I'm glad you came. They'll be down from the barn in a while and I'll put on some more pancakes. Unless you're hungry now?"

"No, just coffee if you have some."

As the two women chatted about the winter, the sugaring, the old farm house, Clair softened. Her straight brown hair hung in a circle around her face, bangs reaching nearly to her eyes, concealing much of the structure of her face. She was a shy, solitary woman who usually put off meeting people or situations until they became inevitable, and she had been surprised at herself when she invited Anna down to the farm last week. Clair wondered all week what they would talk about if Anna came. It was not that she couldn't talk; she and her friend Elizabeth lived common lives, spoke every day about their children, the weather, the land. Clair looked carefully into the new face across from her own, trying to find its age. She's young, Clair thought, can't be more than thirty.

"What?" she asked, as Anna paused. "I'm sorry, I was listening for the kids upstairs. What were you saying?"

Anna smiled briefly and then her face pulled down again. "I was just saying I'm glad my house is small. It heats easy, but really, it's been such a long winter sometimes I think I just can't haul another log in for the fire." She sighed deeply with a weariness that seemed more profound than the circumstance.

Clair nodded and got up to reach for the coffee pot. She liked listening to Anna talk. Her words seemed soft, blurred, not crisp and hard like these Vermont voices.

"Are you – " she began.

"Are these – " Anna said at the same moment. They laughed at their awkwardness, then Anna stretched her long body and gestured to the paintings hanging around the kitchen and in the dining room. "Are these your paintings?"

"Yes," Clair said, "yes, I did some painting when we were living in New Jersey."

Anna sat for a moment in silence, comfortable with just looking more fully at each of the paintings hanging near her. Suddenly, she heard a noise out on the porch, feet stamping – rapid, staccato – and then the door flew open and a woman blew in, shaking the snow from her hair and parka.

"Brrr." She crossed to where Anna and Clair sat at the table and leaned down to give each a quick hug. "Are you nuts, or what, to be out for a ride in a snowstorm?"

"At least it's warm enough to snow," Anna insisted lightly. But she was embarrassed for a moment. Had it been foolish to come? Was her need for company so obvious? She shook off the fear. Hadn't Elizabeth called her twice in the last week to come and have dinner and keep her company while Tom was on the road?

"How are you?"

"Oh, fine," Elizabeth shrugged off the question. "Three of the kids have been out of school with the flu."

"Oh, no!"

But Elizabeth was laughing. "Don't worry. If they're still sick tomorrow I'll lock them in a bedroom with the t.v. so don't think this means you can't come over to dinner anyway."

Anna looked pleased. "But will Tom go on the road during sugaring?"

"Oh, sure. This is my project, not his. I'll be coming down to help Paul with the collecting."

Anna smiled with pleasure at the two women. It was nice to have company, and here were these women – friends – leading lives that seemed to satisfy them. And Clair painted. She hadn't realized that. The canvases she could see looked ambitious, and had a recognizable style from one painting to the next. And Elizabeth was. . . what? What could be so special about a thirty-six year old divorced woman with five kids? Soon to be divorced, Anna corrected herself, divorced from her lawyer husband, but living now with a boyfriend — she and all five kids and a boyfriend. The boyfriend seemed a bore. But still, Anna dismissed the complaint, Elizabeth did seem special to her, very special. She found comfort in Elizabeth's firm, compact body, her air of competence, of having everything under control. That was what had drawn Anna to her side at the counter of the feed store last month, that and a glimpse of Elizabeth's startlingly blue eyes when she tossed her hair back from her face with a careless gesture of her hand.

"Where did you all come from?" Anna asked suddenly. Then embarrassed by her enthusiasm, "I mean, how could I have lived here this long and not have met you?" She turned to Clair. "Have you and Paul been up here long? We're neighbors and I've hardly even seen you at the store or anything."

Clair looked slightly startled. She's joking, she told herself. She doesn't mean that, about not seeing you. Her voice was soft, her humor self-deprecating, as she explained how she and Paul moved north three years ago this spring. They were tired of living in the city. Paul didn't want to work for a brokerage firm, he wanted to get back to the land, live the way his grandparents had. And she had agreed. They needed a change. Now, with practice, Clair could tell the story Paul's way, begin even to half believe the reality she was creating. Once in a confidence, she had told Elizabeth about the strange loss of funds in the brokerage house, the grand jury indictment against Paul that was never opened to the public. Their sudden move. When Paul told the story of their move, he made it seem natural , like he always wanted to farm. Clair could never remember him talking about that back then, just about the business, getting ahead, getting enough, getting. . . but that didn't matter now. They were here, in Vermont, farming. Couldn't their lives before be anything they wanted them to be?

". . . and you should have seen us that first summer," Clair heard her own voice saying. She enjoyed telling this part of the story. "We arrived in March and took over the whole herd. We bought sixty milking cows without ever milking one first to see what it was like. So we *just* got the milking machine figured out when it was June and the hay was ready to be cut. Paul had memories, I guess, of what a wonderful time haying was, hard work and all, you know, but lots of people helping and having fun. He had a couple of neighbors ready to help and both kids."

"So there we were," Clair gestured broadly to the snow covered field just beyond the driveway. "The hay was cut and ready to bale. We kept both girls out of school, got all set for a day's work. I cooked a turkey to have for lunch and made huge vats of iced tea. Then Paul and old John Clark walked through the fields and decided the hay wasn't ready yet. It needed two more days to dry. Can you imagine?" The three women laughed.

"God, I can just see it," Anna groaned. "But you know, when I came up here I thought maple syrup came straight out of the trees and into the cans."

That was nice of her, Clair thought, accepting Anna's complicit naivete.

"But at *least*," Elizabeth interrupted, "you didn't try to make a living selling maple syrup. Tell her what happened next."

Clair nodded, her eyes still laughing. "Next it rained for two weeks. Paul turned the hay three times before we thought we could put it up. The first time he took the baler out in the field, the entire rig got bogged down in a mudhole." Keep it short, she told herself, don't go on and on. But Anna's face seemed interested and laughingly sympathetic. "It took three tractors to pull us out of that one. We met our neighbors real quickly." She nodded at Anna. "The ones who owned tractors, that is."

"I can see why I've missed you," Anna admitted. "I didn't have a tractor, just a horse." She pushed her chair back and walked over to stand by the wood stove. "Can I put another log on?" The kitchen felt warm and friendly to her, and she found something to envy in this warmth, something that made her welcome and lonely at the same time. She reached into the woodbox and pulled out the heavy piece of split oak, placed it toward the back of the fire. Her body moved smoothly, almost effortlessly and the two women at the table watched. She *is* young, Clair thought, I used to be able to move like that too.

"You're tall, Anna," Elizabeth said suddenly. "When I reach into that woodbox I nearly disappear. Paul built it for six-footers only."

Anna looked pleased. "Hey, I'm only five-ten. I'm the short one in the family. Both my sisters made six foot." She sounded proud of their stature. "You know," she said, giving her voice a mocking tone, "I think I'd probably still have a job if I weren't so tall. I'm a foot taller than my chairman and I don't think it's my poems he hates, he just doesn't want to have to walk down the hall next to me."

"Really?" Elizabeth leaned forward eagerly. She wanted to know more about what had happened to Anna, but it was so hard to ask, straight out, well, why did they fire you? "Do you really think that made a difference? Is he that hung up on how short he is?"

"Oh, I don't know," Anna shrugged, ready to dismiss it. She turned back to the stove, poking the logs with the old wrought iron poker, masking her face from Clair and Elizabeth, but Clair seemed not to notice her reticence.

"Well, why would he have hired you?" she asked curiously. "Didn't he know how tall you were?"

"Really, Clair, you don't put that on a resume," Elizabeth said impatiently. Clair slid back into her chair, pulling away from the table slightly.

"No, you don't," Anna admitted. "But I did have an interview. It's just that I was already sitting down when he came into the room." Her lip curled impertinently. "And frankly, when he got up to walk out, I knew I was in trouble." Her pause was dramatic. "He was wearing two inch stacks on his cowboy boots."

Clair felt the laughter pushing out of her chest, relieving the tension, pulling her more fully into the room, into Anna's and Elizabeth's company. "Oh, god," she gasped after a minute. "That's so funny. Isn't it? And men think we're vain. Can you believe it?"

Anna came and sat back down at the table, comforted. She was realizing she had been lonely for a long while. Some of the weight of that grief of losing her job, her feeling of loneliness and isolation, began to lift as she sat easily now, joking with Clair and Elizabeth about men, their vanity, weakness. She watched Elizabeth's hands clench around the coffee cup as she laughingly described Tom's mornings.

"He thinks he's a rabbit. He always wakes up with a hard-on. About thirty seconds, it's over and he's human again."

"Oh, just wait till he's forty," Clair dismissed her with a wave of a hand. "Then you'll have to listen to him worry about why it doesn't stand up by itself in the morning. Then you have to reassure him, every half hour, about how virile and attractive he is."

Anna laughed with the others, but did not speak. She thought she could see the strain in Elizabeth's hands, meant to be masked by the lightness of her voice. Anna had come to Vermont alone, leaving, with some relief, the city and a relationship behind her. She and Charles seemed to agree on the separation months before it happened, arranging their lives on differing schedules. She rose earlier and earlier so she would have the house to herself and went to bed hours before he was ready, feigning sleep when she heard him come into the bedroom. Yet when she told him she was accepting the job and really leaving, the separation was bruising. She realized, later, she should have let him leave her, or forced him to leave her. The nonchalance with which she had shrugged and started to pack drove him into a fury.

"Two years," he had screamed as she sorted through the records, "aren't you even a little upset?"

"Of course I am," she had lied. But it was the confrontation itself that upset her. She had not slept with a man since.

She was frowning into her coffee mug now, shoulders hunched, slipping back into her own reverie.

"Anna?" Elizabeth was leaning over her. Anna felt a touch on her hand and looked up into Elizabeth's frank stare. "Earth calling Anna, earth calling Anna, come in please," she laughed, imitating her six year old's favorite joke. Anna smiled. The hand was warm. Calloused with work and rough, but warm, firm. Anna rubbed the back of Elizabeth's hand and started to speak.

"Oh, goodness," Clair jumped up from the table. "I hear them coming down from the barn. I hope the pancake batter will still be alright. Elizabeth," she said sharply, "put some more water on for fresh coffee."

"O.K.," Elizabeth released her hand from Anna's and paused, smiling for a moment. Then she turned and joined Clair's hurried preparations.

"How many are we getting ready for, anyway?" Anna asked.

"The new ranger came to have a look at Paul's evaporator," Clair said. "He's got some new gizmo on it to show off. And there are two or three other people with him."

As she listened to the voices out on the porch and the stamp of feet knocking snow off of boots and clothes before coming into the kitchen, Clair put her hand out to rest on the smooth surface of the stove. She took a deep breath and made her mind go quiet for a moment. Then she picked up the bowl of pancake batter and began to stir it slowly. No need to rush. They'd want to talk first when they came in, have some coffee. Clair went to the refrigerator and took out the blueberries she had thawed to add to the batter. Good, she thought. Remembered that. With half her attention she folded the bluepurple berries and juice into the creamy yellow batter, while another part of her imagined forgetting the berries, finding them two days later in the bowl, tasting like stale refrigerator air.

Paul opened the kitchen door and hurried the others into the room. Clair sensed him move across the kitchen.

"Hi, hon," he put his hands on her hips and nuzzled a cold nose behind her ear. "How's it going?"

"Fine," she said brightly, smiling up at his frost reddened face. "You've got ice in your moustache." Her casual voice was denied by her stiff back, the rigid muscles under his hands, which he seemed not to notice. Stop checking on me, Clair thought angrily.

"Need any help?"

"Let's see." Clair looked around the kitchen vaguely as she tilted the melting butter into the cast iron skillet. It sizzled on the hot iron. About ready. "You could pour the water through the coffee, Paul. It's just about to boil."

"O.K. I'll be right back, just want to say hello to folks." He moved across the room, rubbing his chapped hands together.

Anna sat at the far end of the kitchen table, leaning back, her hands behind her head, long legs crossed casually. Taking up space, she noted, smiling. She said hello and was introduced, but none of the men came to sit on her side of the table. They stood clustered awkwardly around the other side, talking to Tom and Elizabeth. Anna watched Elizabeth, her hand on Tom's arm, talk vivaciously to the new ranger – Bob? Pete? Did it matter that she couldn't tell them all apart? Elizabeth seemed to have got it instantly. Anna watched as she radiated energy and warmth through her chatter. No. It wasn't chatter; it seemed important to the men who were listening. They were fascinated, and Elizabeth could be mesmerizing, Anna knew. More than once she herself had been lost in Elizabeth's sharp blue eyes, that strange honeygrey hair.

She saw Paul turn away from the stove and come toward her.

"I don't think we've met," he looked directly at her as he walked over. "You must be Anna and I'm Paul."

Anna sat forward and held out a hand to his. She smiled. "Hi, Paul." He seemed nice. Anna liked the droop at the corner of his eyes, repeated in the ends of his bushy moustache. He seemed kindly, burly, teddybear rough. "How many gallons of syrup did you pour off?"

"Thirty. We didn't lose a drop. And the season's just starting."

Elizabeth heard and turned around. "Thirty! That's great. Pete just said we ought to get at least 300. At $15 a gallon, let's see, that's. . . is that right? We'll have $4500? That's more than $2000 per family. Whoopee." She twirled around, using Tom's arm for a center. "Isn't that fantastic?"

"After expenses," Paul reminded her brusquely. Anna looked at him in surprise, hearing a patronizing and challenging tone in his words that seemed out of place with Elizabeth's light-heartedness. "We have to pay for the tubing and the new evaporator. And I think I'd like to use some propane for the final stages. It's so damn hard to regulate the wood fire. I mean it's a matter on one or two degrees," he explained defensively as Elizabeth started to protest.

"But Paul, the wood is free and we are doing this to make money, remember? The syrup will sell whether it's grade A or A+, O.K.?"

Elizabeth was trying hard to maintain her casual air, but Anna could see she was upset. The money's important to her, Anna reflected, surprised that she had not realized that.

She looked over toward the stove where Clair was piling pancakes out of the frying pans onto a warming platter, wondered if Clair had noticed the argument. Steam was pouring out of the kettle on the back burner.

"Looks like you need a coffee maker. Can I do it? Just pour it through the filter?" Anna asked.

"Yes, thanks. Paul was going to do it, but. . . " she paused. No need to say, but he's fighting with Elizabeth again. "Yes, just pour it through, will you. I think breakfast is ready."

Clair felt Anna's concentration as she poured the water through the filter at a precisely even rate, felt the tension in the room behind her fade in the aroma of fresh coffee and pancakes. Self-confidence and a sense of well-being began to rise in Clair as she looked around now at the warm kitchen, the crackling fire, listened to the hearty voices. A cliche country kitchen, a half ironic voice inside her said, aren't we all having a good time. But Clair rejected the temptation, yes, I am enjoying this. We all are. It's good. As she lifted the last of the pancakes off the skillet, Clair looked around the kitchen again. Details came to her vividly, the long rough-hewn dining table, bright checkered napkins, steaming ceramic coffee mugs. A good morning, she thought, a good morning to remember.

Elizabeth took a platter from Clair. "Pancakes coming up," she announced, "take your seats or I'll pass you by." Tom groaned in mock horror and Anna wondered how he'd got his cue so quickly, watched as Elizabeth raised an eyebrow at him and said, with slight innuendo, "You know I can never get past you." He grinned and grabbed her waist with both hands from behind. "Hey, be careful," Elizabeth said urgently. "My hands are tied up."

"Yeah, perfect," Tom said laughing, running his hands from her waist up to her breasts for a moment before releasing her.

Elizabeth felt her face flush. She saw Paul and the other men watching Tom's hands, looking at her breasts again after he released her. Her eyes were lowered to the pancake platter as she went around the table serving. She could feel the body heat, the rough wool of sweaters and shirts against her jeans as she stood for a moment by each of them. At the end of the table, Anna sat. She was leaning back again.

"Just one," she said, holding out a restraining hand as Elizabeth moved full spatula toward her plate.

"One?" Elizabeth asked cautiously. Why did Anna look so far away? In a lowered voice, "Are you O.K.?"

"Sure. I just don't eat very big breakfasts. I haven't been out working in the barn like all these other folks, you know."

Her eyes looked at Elizabeth; her voice and face were pleasant. But Elizabeth felt her remoteness as if Anna had been sitting on the other side of the large glass window, sitting out there with the bird feeder where the bluejays and grossbeaks perched.

Anna reached for the pitcher of fresh syrup as Elizabeth moved around to the other side of the table and sat down between Tom and Paul. Clair was at the far end talking to the ranger and a fat, jowly man who sold farm supplies. She wasn't really talking, Anna noticed, but listening actively, leaning forward, telling the speaker with her eyes and body that she was listening . Anna tried to listen, too, tried to bypass the conversation at the center of the table and focus her attention on details of which kind of tube was best for collecting sap, which absorbed the most heat the most quickly and started running sooner in the morning. But her attention faded and returned to the center of the table each time she heard Tom's voice. He was bragging and teasing Elizabeth at the same time. It had to do with sex again. And Elizabeth was watching him, playful, indulgent.

Anna glanced away from them. He's disgusting, she thought. She let the anger through for a moment and looked back at Tom's sharp features. He was a handsome man, finer boned than any of the others. His hair was straight, but not thin. Anna was sure he paid very careful attention to how it was cut.

She turned away from the table again, looking out the window behind her to see how much snow had fallen . It was time for her to go home. At the bird feeder the blue jay's head jerked up and down, scattering seed randomly until it found exactly the one it wanted. Anna pushed her chair away from the table and stood to leave.

As she stood, the kitchen door pushed open.

"Oh, good grief," Paul expostulated. "Chip."

"Jesus, man, that last weld on the evaporator must have been a bitch. What took you so long? I think we've eaten the last of the pancakes." Tom's voice was edged with sarcasm.

Chip brushed the snow out of his pale blonde hair and knocked it off his jacket with a glove. When he spoke, his voice was deliberate and slow, as though he refused Tom's taunt. "Ahyeah," he twanged the Vermont assent, "I wanted to get that corner right. No point in having to do it twice."

"For that," Clair said emphatically from the stove, "you get fresh and hot pancakes."

"And my place at the table," Anna chimed in. "I've got to go get Rose out of the snow and get myself back to work."

She moved over toward the door and greeted Chip. She knew him well by now; he worked all winter in her orchard, pruning the trees by himself in the cold grey light. On days when she was home, he came by for a cup of hot tea and a few minutes of talk. It was an interruption she did not mind, enjoying the talk of trees, weather lore, the business of growing apples. Once, he'd taken a winter apple, stored in the bottom of the refrigerator, and cut it across the core to show her the perfect star at the apple's center. He had no special words to appreciate this beauty.

"Isn't that nice?" he'd said and she'd agreed, silently, with a nod. There was an extraordinarily beautiful symmetry in the center of that everyday object. As she learned to know Chip, she learned not to be surprised at his capacity to notice these things as a matter of course and only wondered that he had no system, no framework or context to classify beauty, make it an intellectual apprehension as well as an emotional one.

Anna could tell from his bristliness that Chip was annoyed at having been left in the barn to finish the work while the other men came down to eat. But she also knew he had probably volunteered to finish the job and turned down several offers of help.

"I didn't see Rose," he said to her now, "or I'd have come down sooner. Do you have to go?"

"Yeah, I'd better get to work," Anna grimaced. She didn't say, I'm annoyed. She couldn't understand why she was; it had, after all, been a pleasant visit. But Chip could see she meant to leave. He walked over to the table where Clair had poured him a cup of coffee.

Anna said a general goodby, then turned to Clair to thank her. Clair put down the coffee pot to give Anna a hug. "Come down again. You don't have to wait for an invitation. I'm always here."

"Thanks, I'd like that," Anna agreed. "It's a nice distance to ride Rose." She paused, then said in a lower voice, "And I'd like to talk with you about your painting some time."

Clair hesitated, nodded. "Good. If you'd talk with me about your poems."

"It's a deal." Anna went out of the door smiling.

She strode over to where Rose was tied to a small tree and pulled the snowy saddle blanket off of her. Shaking the blanket with one hand, she reached down to tighten the saddle girth with the other. "Make it easy on me, Rose. Don't hold your breath, O.K.? We're on our way home." Rose nodded, pawing the ground several times in anticipation.

As Anna was turning to mount, she saw the kitchen door open and Elizabeth ran out without a coat. She came toward Anna, her grey shoulder-length hair and grey sweater quickly picking up a dusting of snowflakes. Her eyes, Anna thought, are the only color in this entire landscape. I've never seen eyes that blue.

"You are coming to dinner tomorrow." It was a statement.

"I don't know." Anna realized she didn't know whether she wanted to go or not. "Let me see how my work goes, O.K.?" She looked away from Elizabeth's eyes and mounted the horse.

Elizabeth placed her hand on Rose's neck, then on Anna's thigh. "Please come. I really want you to come." Her voice wasn't pleading, just firm.

"Well," Anna paused. "I'll probably come." She turned Rose and headed out the driveway on a path grown completely unmarked from the snow fallen in the two hours since she had ridden in.

# Chapter 2

"Hey, I get one whole night in my own bed without you getting up to check the g.d. fires," Tom said, looking one last time at the temperature which refused stubbornly to move above the freezing mark. He patted Elizabeth on the ass. "We'll light some other fires, baby."

Paul wandered glumly around the kitchen after they left. "I wonder if that idiot ever speaks except in cliche," he said angrily after a moment.

"What do you mean?" Clair was surprised at his vehemence.

"Light some other fires. Come on baby light my fire. God, what an ass. The man's thirty and he talks like an eighteen year old. I don't see how she can stand it." He jerked open the cabinet door and took out a dusty bourbon bottle, pouring a shot into his half filled cup of coffee.

"Well," Clair ventured, "I do guess I wish he wouldn't touch her that way in front of the children. It doesn't seem right, comfortable, I mean, like he's putting on a show." She wasn't sure now what she had meant to object to.

"Yeah," Paul said briefly. Then, "I wish it would warm up."

"You deserve a night off. It's going to be a long run."

"Yeah," Paul said again. He gathered his coffee and put the Sunday paper under his arm. "Do you need any help?" he asked vaguely, looking around the kitchen.

"I'm fine." Clair followed him with her attention into the living room, listened to him stoke the stove and drop a log in, stretch, sigh, and finally settle into the big chair by the hearth. She rinsed each sticky plate and loaded them in the dishwasher one at a time, her movements methodical. It was Sharon's day to help her with clean-up, but Clair didn't call her down to the kitchen. The solitude of dirty dishes, she had called it years ago, telling Paul angrily, "If I ever want to be left alone all I have to do is start cleaning up the kitchen." She seldom minded the solitude now, indeed had learned to seek it after social interactions.

"Take time for yourself," the therapist told her as she was leaving the hospital. "Take whatever time you need. And ask for help, let others help you if you need it." She felt the concern in his fatherly air as he leaned forward toward her and repeated, "Ask for help. Your husband wants to help you."

It had been hard to disagree with him, hard to express her disbelief in Paul's repeated offers of help, and when she had, she felt his patina of concern shift slightly.

"Do you have any evidence of that?"

Evidence? No, she had no evidence and the question hung in the air like a judgment. Once back at home, Clair could not clearly reconcile the two directions the therapist had suggested — take what you need and ask for help. What she needed most was to be able to do things herself, for herself. She needed more of her own life, more control over her life; so she grasped jealously at those things she could do, and had not been able to ask for help even in exhaustion.

But that was before I met Elizabeth, Clair reminded herself, marvelling how much simpler coping had become now that she had someone to confide in. Clair moved around the kitchen, collecting the butter dish and half empty syrup pitchers, wiping down the kitchen table. She smiled, remembering the night Tom announced boisterously that he had a new girl friend — not that having a girl friend surprised them, he'd had one every six weeks since they'd know him — but that she was a woman with five children. Clair was shocked. How could a woman with children run around with a man like Tom, she wondered? And when Elizabeth had come to live in the rambling old family farm house where Tom had lived alone since his father died, she and Paul had both been dumbfounded.

"Tom likes to be thought of as outrageous," Elizabeth had confided to Clair, "and I'm even more outrageous — in a different way — than Diane was, even with her horrid orange hair and nearly topless dresses.

My husband was so respectable. I think Tom liked that a lot. Of course," she added self-consciously, "he's in love with me, too, but he *is* enjoying the rest of it."

Clair turned the kitchen light off and looked back to check that nothing was forgotten. The kitchen was a serene place now, warm, polished, quiet. Even the fire had quieted, damped back, its energy turned inward. In the living room Paul dozed under the business section. No longer a part of that world, his one indulgence was this Sunday afternoon immersion into stocks and finances. He looked tired, she noticed, and older. The stubble he shaved each morning was grey now, not black, and the skin on the back of his hands was weathered, spotted and aged. She had not seen his hands resting for a long time.

Clair picked up the front page and read the week's headlines with half a mind. This was a better life, she told herself, looking through the catalog of violence, political corruption. It had been a hard transition for both of them — two people in their forties — hard on the kids, too, but they were all settling now. Paul seemed frustrated at times, but there was so much work. His energy seemed less oppressive to her than it had before. She wondered whether she was getting stronger or Paul mellowing.

Clair picked up the Arts section and flipped back to the gallery openings. Just like Paul reading the stock exchange news, she thought guiltily. How nice it would be to have Anna stop by. But she hadn't talked to anyone about her painting in years. She kept those canvases on the wall more as a reminder that she had once painted, than as an identification of who she was now. At times it was even hard to remember why she had wanted to paint, who that person was who filled a pallette with color, turned and set a brush to an empty canvas. She had set up her easel in this house more to convince Paul that she was well, her old self, than because she wanted to paint. Once or twice she fiddled with the tubes of oil, mentally sketched a beginning for herself, but the blankness of the canvas when she faced it overwhelmed her and finally she had taken the canvas off of the stretcher, rolled it and stored it in a closet.

Beside her Paul stirred and sat up.

"Any more coffee?"

"It's on the stove."

She heard the door of the cabinet open and close. He came back into the living room, fiddled idly with the stereo tuner for a moment. Clair's own anxiety rose, as he fidgeted.

"Did you enjoy the breakfast?" she asked him finally.

"Hmm? Oh. Yes." He paused. "The pancakes were just fine."

"I mean did you enjoy the people? Wasn't it nice to meet Anna?"

He stared into the fire for a moment. Oh, shit, Clair thought, something is wrong. She felt weary. It was just starting to be O.K. and now something was wrong. Paul shifted in his chair and turned toward her.

"Look. I don't think we ought to have Elizabeth over here any more. I don't like it." His words came out in a rush and he sank back into the chair as though he were deflated.

"What?"

"I don't think we ought to have her over here." He paused and looked back toward the fire. "I just don't like her influence."

"Influence?" Clair's voice rose on a high pitch and then broke. "Influence? Who do you think she is influencing? Sharon is never around here any more. Do you think she'll corrupt Tammie?" She was trying not stammer in her surprise, too surprised to even feel anger.

"Don't be stupid." Paul was irritated out of depression and sat back up, rigid in his chair. "You know what I mean. She just doesn't represent our values."

"But what about the sugaring?" Clair blurted it out.

Paul shrugged his shoulders and seemed to relax, as though she had agreed with him, Clair realized.

"I'll just have to do it myself. It won't be easy, but I can manage." Clair was shaking her head in disbelief. "We've never approved of her, of what she's done. I would think you'd be relieved not to have to deal with that kind of conflict, Clair. It will be a little hard for both of us, but I think it will be the best thing."

Clair was speechless. God, she thought, does he really think he's doing this for me? For my own good?

Paul didn't wait for her to speak. "Honey," his tone was gentle, but final, "she's an immoral person. She's dragged those five kids into the middle of this sex thing with a man who's not worth two cents. It must be upsetting to you. You said so yourself in the kitchen. You said, they're putting on a show. I'll bet," he was suddenly scathing, as he dismissed Elizabeth from their lives, "I'll bet they don't even keep those children out of the bedroom."

Clair held her body still in the chair and stared woodenly into the fire. I must speak rationally to him, she told herself, I must argue with his like an adult and convince him he is wrong. This is something we can negotiate, like adults. As these words repeated over and over she forced her spine against the chair back. She wanted to rock forward, wrap her arm around her chest, rock and console herself. Beyond the fire where her eyes focussed she could feel the emptiness, the danger, feel the wind start to move past her skin and suck the warmth in the room, in her body, into that void. She took a deep breath, looked at the fire, and forced the light back out into the room. She loosened the grip of her hand on the chair arm and turned to look at Paul. He sat forward in his large chair, one arm resting on his knee, looking at her. His face was set in an attitude of concern.

Why Paul's got his worried face on, Clair observed ironically. It was a feature she learned to recognize after she came home from the hospital, an attitude she found him adopting when he felt he ought to respond to her but didn't know how, or perhaps, didn't feel anything, but knew he ought. It was different from his face when he was truly concerned or upset. She was never able to explain the difference to her therapist.

"He's always worried about you," the doctor insisted.

But Clair didn't think so, and now, as she watched him, she realized what the difference was. He's self-conscious about his face; he's arranged it consciously. He's thinking about how his face looks to me.

"Look," he said, "I don't mean to be harsh. Maybe I'm a little too old fashioned." He flashed her a quick, self-ironic smile, and then went back to his worried expression. "But I'm just thinking about us, Clair."

Clair cleared her throat. She thought she could answer him now. "I think Elizabeth always thinks about her children. She loves them very much. She's a wonderful mother and would never do anything to hurt them." The words sounded unconvincing, even to her.

He shrugged. "But with five kids, why would she leave her husband? She didn't have a cent. How could she even feed them?"

"Maybe she felt like the marriage was smothering her. Maybe she felt that she had to get out to survive and that would be better for the children in the long run." Clair's voice was calm now.

"Did she tell you that?"

"Not exactly. And you know how surprised we were about Tom. I mean, how good he seemed with the children." There. He couldn't deny that. They *had* agreed that Tom seemed in his element in the noisy, chaotic house. Months later, when Clair dared to ask Elizabeth how Tom felt about having all those children around, she laughed and said, "Right at home. After all, he was the next oldest of eight, so changing diapers wasn't new to him."

"How did you know that?" Clair marvelled at Elizabeth's prescience in loving such a man.

"Know it? I knew him all my life. And his family, too. There isn't anybody who's always lived here who doesn't know everybody else who's always lived here."

Now Paul was silent, ruminating. Clair could see he hadn't expected her to fight back. What could she offer him?

"Are you angry with her because of the syrup?" Clair asked. "Because she wants to do it her way and not yours?"

Paul made a dismissing motion with his hand. "I'm right," he said abruptly, angrily. "I'm right, you'll see I'm right." He stood up. "I'm going to start the milking."

Clair watched him stride vigorously out of the room and a moment later heard the kitchen door slam. As she gathered small points of repose back into herself, she felt the quiet begin to settle around her again.

That was hardly a negotiation, Clair reflected, feeling nonetheless pleased with herself. She hadn't given in, at least she hadn't given in. But she had never given in to Paul about Elizabeth, she realized with some surprise, and he'd never liked Elizabeth, not from the first.

"She's just not your caliber," he insisted that first night they met her.

"I'm not a rifle, Paul," Clair insisted mildly, "and this is not Jersey. There aren't that many women around here for me to know. I do get lonely, Paul, you know that." He remained silent. What was it, Clair wondered, that he so disliked about Elizabeth?

She remembered their first meeting, Tom's hearty invitation to come over for dinner. When they walked into the formal hallway of his two hundred year old house, Clair suddenly realized that it was not Tom who had invited them, but this new woman. In the two years they lived down the road, he had never asked them to come over. She supposed Paul had been there before on business or something, but this was her first visit. They walked around the formal staircase that rose in front of the entrance and went down the long hall toward the kitchen at the back of the house.

Elizabeth stood at the stove, her back toward them, dressed in a blue sweater and jeans. Clair stood staring. She had grey hair. She could not imagine Tom being involved with an old woman, with a woman who, whatever her age, did not "color" her hair to seem young and with it, to match Tom's self-image. What did we talk about, Clair wondered. She remembered Paul's politeness, his eyes showing a measured disapproval as he moved over to one side of the kitchen to talk business with Tom. We must have found something to say; we were left on our own.

"I meant to charm you," Elizabeth had told Clair after they became friends. "I knew everybody in this village, but nobody wanted to know *me* after I left my husband. There I was, alone in the house all day with the two babies, and only Tom and the kids at night. I needed a woman friend. I decided it would be you." She laughed and touched Clair's arm gently. "It's a good thing you were you; you were easy to charm."

And she had been, Clair remembered, knowing that her own isolation in this new life was at least as extreme as Elizabeth's. Elizabeth is the first friend I've made for myself since I married Paul. Eighteen years and I've finally chosen my own friend. She could not tell Elizabeth this, could not tell her she had chosen her against Paul's inclination, admit to her friend that Paul did not like her. But it was not that Paul had ever really chosen her friends for her, she corrected herself, be honest now. It was that you never could be close to a woman he didn't approve of. You let him choose for you. He'd make some scathing remark about her voice or her way of dressing. Or her mind. And you found someone else.

Clair felt pleased for a moment. To have given in to Paul would have meant giving up a part of herself, and she hadn't given in, even though he was mad at her now. She was uncomfortable with this realization, feeling that he wasn't so mad at Elizabeth any more, but at Clair herself for defending Elizabeth. Surely he would be able to see that she was right, that Elizabeth was a wonderful mother. Clair didn't understand how anyone who saw Elizabeth with her children could believe anything else. As for leaving her husband, Clair didn't think Elizabeth herself knew for sure why she had done that. She remembered Elizabeth telling her once about a horse she and her husband bought, a Morgan colt they hadn't wanted to geld, but use for stud. They fixed a huge box stall in the barn, but he was restless. Even after a day in the fields, he'd come in at night and paw, pace, chew the top rail of the stall door. They put metal on the rail to stop the chewing and padded the walls so he wouldn't hurt himself when he kicked, but all night during that summer Elizabeth could hear him pacing, pacing, the restless energy looking for a way out of the luxurious padded stall.

"We had to get rid of him," she told Clair. "I couldn't stand it. I couldn't sleep at night, listening to him. We couldn't leave him out, either, or he'd clear the fences and be in the next county before dawn. I think I identified with him." She paused and ran her hand through her hair, a reflective gesture Clair had come to recognize. "I think that may have been what my marriage was to me, a padded stall. Padded cell, really." They had talked of other things.

Clair had been startled at those words, padded cell. To Elizabeth, they were just an image, she realized, a cliche. But she knew there were rooms like that at the hospital she had been taken to. Not that she had been put in one. Her room was light and airy, painted creamy white with yellow trim around the barred windows. But she ran all of those words through her consciousness in the days she lay still in the bed. Padded cell. Looney bin. Nut house. Insane asylum. Crazy. Mad. Nervous breakdown. She processed each concept through her own experience, trying to connect her fears with the reality of where she was, what had happened to her.

She didn't often think about that time, but now as she sat looking into the fire she tried to bring back some of the memories of how she had been just before she was taken into the hospital. She remembered the constant anxiety, that same feeling she had this afternoon just before Paul spoke about Elizabeth. Then, too, she had known something was wrong, something bad was coming, but he wouldn't speak to her, wouldn't tell her what it was. She went from day to day, holding his tension inside her, soothing him when he came to her at night, never daring to say to him, "Paul, what's wrong? I think I deserve to know what's wrong." Even the children knew. Even? She corrected herself. They probably knew before me. They feel it sooner, that violence under the surface, the tension that permeates every exchange. It went on for weeks, for months, until she felt so far away from Paul, so far away that when he stood next to her and spoke, she could hardly hear his voice, only the echo of a once familiar tone coming across a long distance. And then she remembered him shaking her, remembered that she had been crying and he was shaking her, but she couldn't hear what he was saying. Not then. Gradually, as the months went by, she began to remember. Even then she was not sure what she remembered and what the doctors and Paul had told her.

She remembered, she thought, that she had read the newspaper that night, remembered reading about the sealed indictment. But Paul told her later that none of her friends would know, that she didn't have to worry about anything, that his name was never in the paper. She wanted to ask, then how did I know it was you? Where did this memory come from? Of me, sitting in the living room before dinner, waiting for your train to come in, waiting for you to drive home. Sharon was setting the table. I remember that. I think she was. And I picked up the afternoon paper. I started to cry. Her eyes watered now, but she blinked the tears away. Yes, something in the paper made me start to cry, but I don't really know what it was. And then I couldn't stop crying. Sharon came into the room and Paul came home and I couldn't stop the tears and Paul was shaking me, but I couldn't stop crying. I cried for days. Clair shook her head ruefully and folded the newspaper lying across her lap. I don't even know what I had to cry about.

She sat in reflective silence, the rough dryness of the newspaper in her hands like a tactile memory. Gradually the everyday noise of the house began to work its way into her consciousness. The fire hissed and sputtered, a cat stretched and yawned on the hearth, upstairs a door slammed. She heard Tammie's steps coming down the stairs and picked up the newspaper to look occupied.

"Hey, Mom," came her voice from the kitchen, "do I have time to feed the goats before dinner?"

Dinner? Clair was surprised. Was it that late? "Sure, honey. I haven't even started it."

She stood up and walked toward the window. The slate grey sky had never really been daylight, but now even the lighter shades of darkness were beginning to fade. Lights were on in the barn and the milking parlor. She could not see the hill behind the barn where the maple trees stood, long dark hoses protruding from their trunks instead of collecting pails. As she watched, the remaining light filtered out of the sky and closed down the landscape. Time to fix another meal. Clair turned and went back into the kitchen.

# Chapter 3

Elizabeth turned over sleepily and felt Tom's hand move up between her thighs. She moved closer to him, running one hand over his smooth, muscled chest and nuzzling her face into his neck and shoulder, loosening her thighs, waiting for his hand to move higher. But now he dozed with his hand in her crotch. She reached down and pressed it further into her, shifting her hips, beginning to feel her breasts tingle. Tom felt her movement, pulled his hand away and rolled over on top of her. Elizabeth let her legs part, then said, irritated, "Play with me a little, for god's sake , Tom."

"Mmmrrff," he mumbled, pretending not to hear.

He can't really be snoring in my ear, she thought angrily as she felt him start to penetrate her. No man can fuck while he's unconscious.

"Tom," she said, slipping away from him and trying to push his shoulders up away from hers. "Tom, I said I'm not ready yet."

"Jesus," his eyes were open now and she felt him try to knee her legs apart. "We used to wake up so nice. What's the matter with you this morning, baby?"

Yelling at him would not get her what she wanted, Elizabeth knew. "Look, sweetheart, I want it to be nice. Let's just take it a little slower." She nibbled his ear and ran her tongue around its rim. "You know what I like you to do. . . you're so good. Do that for a minute, then I want you inside me." She slid her hand under his body and caressed the tip of his penis. Resigned, challenged, Tom shifted his weight and played his mouth across her breasts, sucking each nipple hard for a moment, then flicking his tongue back and forth across the hardening tip. Elizabeth felt her thighs start to warm with sensation. Thank god. It never took that long, but it infuriated her when Tom ignored her. She pushed hard on his penis with her thumb and manipulated her own clitoris with the rest of her hand. Elizabeth hated having to talk about sex. She wished Tom would know her body better, but she had never been able to talk to him about it.

"O.K.?" he asked perfunctorily, raising his head from her breast.

"Mmm," Elizabeth murmured, and he slid into her at once.

While Tom got up to dress, Elizabeth remained curled for a moment in the warm bed, watching him move from dresser to closet. As a teenager, she had always imagined a man like this for herself — a perfect body, tall, strong-shouldered, lean, the way the cowboys in the cigarette ads must look under their loose workshirts and faded denims. She cuddled into the pillows pulling Tom's heavy musky scent closer toward her. She wondered why sex in her fantasies had always been so much more exciting, rewarding, than in real life. Lying with her head on his pillow, she remembered how as a girl she had imagined sex was all that adults thought about, that given the permission to be sexual, it would become an overwhelming obsession. Elizabeth sighed. She still felt desire, but there was so little time now to think about satisfying it.

Tom came back into the bedroom. "Artie's crying," he announced, "and I gotta get going out of here."

Elizabeth reluctantly slid out from the warmed bed and wrapped a terry cloth robe around her. "He's got a rash again. They all get it in the winter. It's just too cold to let him run around with it all hanging out and that's the only way to cure it."

She scuffed barefoot down the hall to the baby's room where she could hear Artie's low wail. "Hey fella," she said, picking him up and heading toward the warmer bathroom. "Ain't it kind a hard to holler with your thumb in your mouth?" Artie blinked at her appreciatively as she stripped off his soaking wet diaper and bathed his red, irritated bottom with warm water. "Eighteen months, Arthur. Don't you have any urges toward maturity yet little one?"

"What's 'turity, Mom?" asked three year old Colin, wrapping the tie of Elizabeth's bathrobe around her knees.

"It's getting up in the morning by yourself and using the bathroom to pee, like you do, instead of peeing in your diaper," Elizabeth explained patiently. "Colin, go see if the girls are up yet and wake up Larry. I want everybody downstairs pronto. Tell them we aren't going to keep the school bus waiting this morning, O.K.?"

Colin scooted importantly out of the bathroom, bouncing off Tom's legs as he rushed in and started to shave. Elizabeth sat down on the toilet and finished pinning Artie's diapers.

"How is he?" Tom peered at her through the mirror.

"Sore. Where are you working today?"

"South." His gaze shifted to his raised chin in the mirror as he ran the electric razor over it.

"Oh." Elizabeth made her voice cautiously pleased, then asked casually, "So any chance you'll sleep back here tonight?" During their first months together Tom had found many ways to arrange his travelling so they could have an extra night or two together during the week.

"Don't know," Tom began noncommittally, "there's a. . . "

"Mom, please," Shanna interrupted, crossing one leg over the other as she came into the bathroom and assuming a pained stoop. "I have to pee sooo bad."

"O.K., sweetheart, it's all yours," Elizabeth stood up, raised the toilet cover with the hand that wasn't holding Artie and then shepherded Shanna over to the toilet, hoping she would make it all the way. "Good," she said, tousling the six year old's curly black hair. "Then get dressed. I'm going down to put out breakfast."

Elizabeth stopped in her bedroom, pulled on long underwear, top and bottom, then her jeans and sweater. Every movement was quick and efficient. Without stopping to brush her hair or look in the mirror, she picked up Artie again and went down to the kitchen. Before stoking the fire, she put the kettle on for coffee. Then she plopped Artie in a high chair and began to stir up the coals. Mornings she put herself on automatic in order to get everyone out of the house. She scarcely seemed to have time for conscious thought as she moved between stove and refrigerator, giving Artie a cracker and cup of milk, setting out boxes of cereal and bowls, filling the toaster, warming the frying pan for eggs. One part of her attention noticed that she could hear no noise coming from Larry's room. She grabbed the kitchen broom, went over to the far corner and started to bang the ceiling with the broom handle.

"Let's move it, Larry, I want to hear some sounds up there right now or else." She paused. She heard his feet hit the floor, then silence. "More than that," she hollered at the mute ceiling, "I want you down here in three minutes." She pounded the ceiling again for good measure and then went back to the stove. She shook her head ruefully. Larry was his father's child. The only one of the five, really, who took more after Edward than after her. He hated anything physically difficult: hated cold mornings, hated doing barn chores. Just like his father, Elizabeth reflected, as her oldest child banged through the back kitchen door, eyes sparkling, cheeks reddened with cold.

"Mom, guess what down in the barn? I think Matilda's eggs are hatching!"

"Oh, no. She can't. It's too soon. It's too cold. Pam, how can you tell?" Elizabeth hoped the child was wrong. All she needed to deal with was an incubator.

Pam shrugged, "I don't know. Maybe they aren't." She had expected her news to be greeted with excitement, not distress, and turned to the kitchen table where she poured cereal into bowls for herself and Colin.

"Oh, well, I'll check it in a bit. It's probably all right." She could see Pam's disappointment. "Look, honey, after you put some milk on Colin's cereal, will you run upstairs and see what's happened to Larry? I haven't heard him come back from the bathroom yet. See how he's doing, O.K.?" She cracked two eggs in the sizzling frying pan as she heard Tom start down the stairs.

Elizabeth's attention followed him down the stairs and into the kitchen but she did not turn from the stove when he entered. She put two more eggs in the pan, salted them, and fussed at the edges with a spatula. At the table Tom poured cereal, then came over to the stove for the coffee pot. He seemed not to have noticed her silence, Elizabeth thought, but after a sip of coffee, he leaned on the stove next to her.

"Like I was saying, there's a sales meeting in Bennington this afternoon and if it goes late, I'll just put up there."

"O.K." Elizabeth was casual as she turned the eggs. "I just wondered. I asked Anna to come over this evening and if you were coming home. . . " her voice drifted off as she put the eggs on his plate and held it toward him. If he were coming home. She really didn't know how to finish that sentence, she realized. Did she want him to come home early tonight? Or did she want to see Anna? He didn't give her time to ponder.

"Well, what do you mean?" He gestured with his coffee mug, then sauntered towards the table. "Would it interrupt your girltalk if I came back tonight?" He asked the question with a self-assured grin as he sat down in his place at the head of the table.

"Well," Elizabeth took a sip of her coffee. Careful now, something warned her. "We do talk confidentially, you know," she said, looking up at him from under her eyebrows.

"Confidentially!" he laughed. "I know what you talk about. Isn't having it better than talking about it?" His grin seemed like a wall to Elizabeth, barring communication. She shrugged and gave in.

"You know I always want you home, honey," she said, crossing to where he was seated and running her hands through his thick soft hair. "It's just that if you were going to be home for dinner tonight, I'd have Anna some other night. You know. To keep me company, so I don't forget I'm a grown-up by the time you come back."

Elizabeth went back to the stove as Larry straggled sleepy-eyed into the kitchen and sat down grumpily at the table next to Tom.

"Good morning, bright eyes," Tom quipped, passing the cereal over to him, then pouring it into his bowl when Larry didn't respond.

"Well, I've got to go." He pushed his chair back and stood up, crossing to where Elizabeth stood. "Look, I know I won't be back for dinner. There's dinner at the meeting. But I may cut out afterwards. I've got to be up in Essex Junction first thing in the morning. I'll just play it by ear, O.K.?"

"Fine," Elizabeth agreed with a smile. It was the first time in several months he'd even thought about coming back during the week. "Fine. I'll warm the bed up for you." She pulled his head down toward her and gave him a lingering kiss. "Have a good day."

"Yeah, you too."

"I guess I'll go ahead and have Anna come over then," she called to his parting back.

Elizabeth was pleased and slightly excited. But there was no time now for reflection. She filled three lunch bags with sandwiches from the freezer, added apples and cookies, stacked the bags next to each child's pile of books, then started pulling on boots and warm-up pants, zipping jackets. Spring couldn't come soon enough, she thought for the hundredth time, as she tried to work the cheap plastic zipper on Shanna's parka.

"Go on out, Pam, and let us know when the bus starts down the hill."

In ten seconds Pam was back. "It's already coming down the hill, Mom, and Larry doesn't even have his boots on yet," she exclaimed self-righteously.

"All right, Larry, move." Elizabeth was angry now and he began to look awake for the first time. "I will not have that bus waiting for you every morning. I want you out in the yard instantly. There's just no excuse for this." She kissed Shanna and Pam who tumbled out into the unshoveled snow. Larry looked sullen and resentful as she handed him his lunch and books and propelled him forward toward the door.

"Look at me," she commanded.

He complied, still reluctant, his lower lip jutting out and down, tears at the corners of his eyes.

"O.K." She relented. He looked so put-upon, she thought. How could any child so resent getting up in the morning? "Give me a kiss, Larry, then I want you to run all the way to the road. Will you?"

He nodded and she closed the door behind him, not watching to see whether or not he obeyed.

Elizabeth sat at the breakfast table with a cup of hot coffee, musing, watching Colin try to build a wall of blocks around Artie, who uncooperatively knocked them over with his foot. It frustrated and amused her—how like Larry was to his father. As a child she had always loved physical sensation, seeking it out until she was sweaty and bone tired. Even as an adult physical labor was a pleasure to her. Elizabeth thought Edward's disinclination to physical work and sports was merely preoccupation with his career. But as she watched Larry grow, she began to realize that she and Edward would always live separately.

She knew women for whom that would have been fine, but for Elizabeth there had been a profound frustration in not having Edward's immediate approval and support. When she had showed him – with pride – how firm her muscles were after the birth of their first child, he'd frowned.

"You think too much of such things," he warned. "Women shouldn't be so concerned about that."

What did that mean? Elizabeth had wondered and she had been angry for days without knowing why.

She supposed – thinking of her anger at Tom this morning–that she should be grateful that he seemed to like sex with her. But at the same time, she was afraid they were losing that pleasure. After a year together, sex was perfunctory. She felt Tom performing with only a little more enthusiasm than he brushed his teeth. She had thought he was angry with her for stopping him this morning. He *had* been annoyed, she couldn't doubt that, brusque and fairly careless of her when he got out of bed and during their conversation while he was shaving. Conversation. She smiled at the memory of Shanna's tousle-headed urgency.

But he had said he might come home tonight. She was pleased. How had that happened? Elizabeth did not think of herself as a complicated person and she did not ascribe complicated motives to others. When she first began the involvement with Tom she realized that the things that pleased him were fairly simple and mundane. He was not an intelligent man and he was not sensitive; but she had seen in him a kind of generosity she had not found in her wealthy professional husband, and she preferred Tom's easy going, easy to read, nature to Edward's selfishness and jealousy. Sexually, Tom *had* wanted to please her, something that had never occurred to Edward. At least at first Tom had wanted to please her, and perhaps this morning had reminded him of that.

Another possibility occured to her which made her uncomfortable – vaguely stirred some deep part of her to which she had no access, no images or vocabulary with which to express it – and so when she did contemplate it, she treated it lightly. She thought perhaps she and Anna would even laugh together tonight and she imagined saying lightly, "I think Tom's jealous of you," and she would wait for Anna's laughing response. "Oh, right," Anna would drawl, mockingly, and they would talk of other things, but talk, Elizabeth sensed, with heightened excitement.

In pleasant anticipation, Elizabeth got up and began clearing the breakfast table. The sky was still overcast, but she hummed cheerfully, content to be where she was, doing the work she was doing. Artie had curled up inside Colin's fortress with his thumb in his mouth and seemed about to take his morning nap. Colin, pleased with this passivity, was building an elaborate edifice over his fortress's gate. Elizabeth stacked the dishes in the sink and turned to clear off the stove. Eggs. Eggs. Oh, my god, she thought, I forgot about Matilda.

"Colin," she said hastily, "I have to go out to the barn for a minute. You and Artie stay right here in the kitchen."

"Oh shit, shit. I should have gone out as soon as the school bus came. What if they've hatched? Maybe Pam was wrong." She pulled on a wool jacket as she ran the hundred yards to the barn. Inside the pen, a large grey goose stood in a far corner.

"Matilda, why aren't you on your nest?" Elizabeth spoke sharply to the goose and was answered by a nervous honk. She bent over the nest and saw that several of the eggs had been cracked by goslings trying to work their way out, but she could see no sign of movement now. She went into the feed room and got a box to put the nest into, knowing that something was wrong with the goose and she could not be counted on to return to her cold nest now.

"Oh, Matilda," Elizabeth moaned, "how could you let me down like this? You're supposed to know how to do this, how to be a mother. What's wrong with you?" She gathered the hay around the eggs and lifted the entire nest into the box. The goose would not come near her, seemed to take no interest in Elizabeth's ministrations. As she stood to carry the box into the house, she saw a tiny fluff of fur by her foot, half hidden under the hay. She stooped again and pick up a tiny gosling who had broken out of the egg and wandered away from the nest. Its beak and feet were transparent with frostbite, looking almost like a plant leaf that melts in the cold. She put the gosling on the nest and — weeping — carried the box into the house.

# Chapter 4

Anna poured the bucket of water into Rose's trough and reached for the grain scoop. The temperature had dropped during the night and it was one of those mornings when everything that wasn't yet frozen solid steamed—the horse's coat, the fresh water, Anna's breath on the metal cold air. She was tired and moved slowly, her limbs resisting the extra effort necessary on such a morning.

"I wish I didn't have to go to work this morning, Rose. But then again," she paused and looked at the ice water running down the horse's whiskers as she raised her muzzle out of the water, "I'm glad I'm not a horse." She shivered, picked up the empty bucket and headed through the snowdrifts back to the house. About eight inches of new snow covered her car and weighted the branches of the rows of apple trees leading up the hill. She started the car to warm it and went back into the house for a last cup of coffee.

She had begun the school year in a burst of energy and high spirits. Fall was a wonderful season in the orchard. It seemed that she walked out of her house each morning into translucent golden sunshine, sun which was reflected in the red and gold of ripening fruit. Anna had been in awe of the abundance, the enormity of each small tree bearing so many hundreds of apples. Originally her house had been a tenant house belonging to the orchard, grown too small now to house the dozens of workers required for the harvest; too small even for Chip and his wife and daughter, though it would have been convenient, situated as it was nearly in the center of the orchard.

Now Anna swept the snow off of her car and watched the large dollops of snow drop like ripe fruit off the branches around her. Each fall for three years she had come out to her car each morning, swung her briefcase onto the front seat and reached over and picked three or four apples to snack on during the day. She ate one as she made the fifteen minute drive to the college, marvelling how quickly the sun had warmed one side of the apple, leaving the night's chill on the other. But the abundance of autumn had been no precursor of this winter, when it seemed the sun never rose in the morning and there was no warmth anywhere outside the ten foot radius of th cabin's little wood stove.

Anna flung her briefcase into the passenger seat, knocked the snow off her boots and slid into the ancient rusted Volvo. Damn. She slammed the door and it bounced open again, frozen. She slammed the door again, ineffectually, then again and again. Finally she climbed out of the car, slammed the door from the outside, leaning her weight against it. There. It caught. She went around to the passenger's side, opened the door and slid through to the driver's seat.

"Betsy," she announced to the car, "I think you and I may be about to come to a parting of ways." She sighed and adjusted the hand choke. "Either that or this winter has got to come to an end."

She backed the car out into the unplowed snow and headed down the long driveway. Chip would plow before she had to drive back in and getting out was usually easy since she lived at the top of a long hill. For generations, the orchard had dominated the hill, flanked by several farms on the lower reaches. When Anna turned out of her driveway, she headed down the road toward one of the bridges that spanned the creek branch rambling along the base of the hill. This morning the beauty was not visible to her; preoccupied by Monday morning weariness, she could not focus on the austere frozen landscape through which she travelled.

Instead, as she drove, her thoughts turned toward the college, toward the class she had to teach that morning on Wordsworth. She had spent an hour the night before trying to focus on the text of the short poem she assigned for today's class and had been almost unable to read it. She finally put the book down, consoling herself with the thought that she must know more about Wordsworth than her sophomore students. She could start with an introduction to Romanticism, then read the poem out loud. Class discussion usually animated her, brought her out of the strange ennui that threatened to overtake her during the last weeks. Textual analysis, she decided as she poured a small glass of brandy to take to bed, I can always do a textual analysis of the poem after I've read it to them.

The problem, she knew, was that whenever she began to prepare her classes, grade papers, even write in her journal, her mind immediately switched into a rerun of the scenario in her chairman's office just before Christmas break. It recurred vividly, seemed complete in every detail, and never failed to evoke in her the same emotional response – a grief and shame before which she was defenseless. She had not been able to tell anyone what he had said to her, but she retold the scene to herself again and again, chastising herself for not having handled it better, not having had at hand the response which would have refuted his accusations, proved to him that her work was, after all, satisfactory.

When her department chairman asked to see her on the last morning of classes, Anna was not alarmed. She was tired after a long semester, exhausted from demanding classes and students. For a year now, she had been experimenting in her classes with ways of involving her students in their own learning, letting them select the material they needed to study and the ways in which they would study it. It began during her first January term when she was teaching an intensive course in women poets. How to plan it, she worried, when there were so many poets and she didn't know what the students would want or expect. She relied on her own expertise and walked into the class the first day without a syllabus, asking the students what they knew about women poets and what they wanted to know. She loved the freedom of that approach, but knew when Frank, the chairman, asked her for a copy of her syllabus halfway through the month that he was not pleased with her tactic.

"Aren't there certain poets that have to be included?" he asked. "You can't rely on what amateurs know."

Anna was convinced that her students' search for what they wanted to know was as important as the actual learning, but she knew Frank was not pursuaded.

"Come in, Anna," he had said when she knocked at his half-opened door. "Shut the door, would you?" He sat without rising in his swivel desk armchair and gestured toward the low lounge chair on the other side of the room. Anna's students had joked with her about this arrangement, insisting that the only way he could look down on anybody was by making them sit practically on the floor. Anna folded herself reluctantly into the uncomfortable sagging chair.

"What's happening, Frank?" she smiled up at him confidently.

"Ah, well, ah. The news is not good, Anna." He swiveled uncomfortably in his chair.

"What?" Her heart sank, but she had no idea what he meant.

"I'm sorry to have to tell you that the department has decided not to renew your contract after this year." He paused and cleared his throat, not meeting her eyes. When she did not speak, he glanced at her quickly, then continued. "We, ah, feel that while your work here has been satisfactory, it has not been outstanding and that, ah, you would perhaps be more in your element at another college." He stopped speaking.

Anna stared at him, unblinking. Her peripheral vision seemed to fade away and all she could see was his face—the urbane, chubby self-satisfaction let through no real concern, only a slight discomfort. She stared at his face as though it were an anchor as, for a moment, everything shifted in the office around her. Finally she realized she was meant to speak. He was looking at her now, expectantly. She tested her voice.

"I don't understand. Have my students complained about my courses? About my teaching?" Her throat was dry and her voice sounded thin, pulled out of her.

"No, no, it's nothing like that." Frank was hearty now, jovial in his reassurance. "It's just that at certain times the department must look at the work of its junior staff and evaluate his or her position in our overall pattern, in the scheme of things, you know." He was nodding his head to encourage her understanding while he spoke.

"And I just don't fit in?" The bitterness in Anna's voice was a challenge. Frank pushed his chair back from her a bit and responded coolly, without pretense of concern.

"Well, I'd just say that we feel the promise we saw in you three years ago hasn't come to fruition."

He was looking directly at her now. What in the world does that mean, Anna wondered? She moved uncomfortably in the chair, trying to keep her leg from sticking up unceremoniously under his scrutiny.

"But Frank," she began, after a moment's reflection, "I've just had a new series of poems accepted for publication in the *The New England*

*Journal*. You know that. I showed them to you last month after they were accepted." The surface of her mind refused to move, but under the layer of shock, Anna could hear a faint warning, a memory of the hesitation she felt when she handed those poems to Frank.

"Yes, well," he laughed slightly, "you know Gilbert and I have never agreed about literary merit, and I'm afraid I found those poems, well, weaker than they should have been. And too personal. There's such a fine line," she could see that he was lecturing now, more comfortable as he launched the familiar words, "such a fine line between the personal detail that communicates the universal and the personal event that obscures. . . "

Anna half listened as his voice droned on, trying to collect her thoughts, unable to believe what he was saying, aware even in her astonishment at what was happening to her, that she was in part the victim of Frank's "gentlemen's disagreement" with Gilbert Stewart, himself a mediocre poet, but more prestigious than Frank in his role as editor of a pretentiously intellectual literary journal. Shit, she protested to herself, those were good poems. But you knew he wouldn't like them, another voice insisted. How could you have expected him to like them when you know how he feels about those things? For the center poem in the series was a long narrative about her grandmother's death – in the thirties when Anna's mother had only been a girl – from a self-induced abortion. The narrator in the sequence was trying to come to terms with the contradictions in this act of defiance which became self destruction, trying to find the meaning of defiance in her own life. Of course he thought the poems were too personal. How could she have expected anything else?

"Well," she could tell he was beginning to conclude now, "I hope this won't be too painful. We expect you'll find another job without any problem. After all," he smiled condescendingly, "you are a very personable young woman. And don't let this spoil your holidays. Think about where you'd like to be, file some applications, and we'll see you back here in January for the short term." He rose and opened his office door, then retreated to his chair again.

She sat for a moment, not sure what would be an appropriate response, then realized she was meant to leave quietly, which she did. She could not speak, could not trust her voice, and knew that the bitter words running through her head would only make him more uncomfortable, more likely to lash out at her. As she walked down the long corridor toward the exit, she wondered if she should have shown her poems to Frank before she had sent them to the journal, asked his advice about sending them out at all. But that's disgusting, her inner voices said, you know you would never want or need his advice; this was true, but she also knew in that thought that she had been meant to ask, that the expectation that she would ask had been present in Frank's attitude toward her from the beginning.

"Stupid little twerp," she muttered as she strode toward the door, "see you back here for the short term. Where the hell else does he think I'd be?"

Her winter term course in Contemporary Women Writers had filled this year in the first hour of registration. Dozens of students who wanted to take it had been shut out and Anna knew many of them had complained to Frank, wanted to know why he had put a limit of thirty on enrollment, couldn't he get another instructor to offer another section? She flung open the door, her anger propelling her out into the early December dark.

"And *you* only got three students to take your contemproary poets course," she continued angrily. "No wonder he's doing this to me. Aammon, Ashbury, Berryman, Lowell, not a single woman worthy of the honor. Literary merit. Shit." Her body rigid, she stomped toward the car.

Not until she sat alone in her car, shielded by the familiar shell-like frame, did the shame overtake her anger. She sat with her head resting on the steering wheel and felt her face flush with shame and embarrassment. She tried to remember what he had said. Why was she being fired? How could she ever tell her father? What should she tell people? People? What could she say to her students? I'm not good enough to teach here? We, we, he kept saying we. Who did he mean? Had the rest of the department really agreed with him? Had they all read her poems and decided—what was it he had said — literary merit? Did they all think she was a bad poet, she wondered. Bob? He had the office next to hers and they went to lunch together twice a week. Wouldn't he have told her? Said something to warn her? And then, how can I go back and work there next month, knowing that's what they think about me?

Now, at the end of February, Anna felt she had aged years in just a few weeks. She did not understand what had happened to her energy, why she always felt tired, like she was swimming underwater, moving against a strange resistance in the air around her.

"Try it again," she could hear her father's voice say, gently, humorously, when she had not gotten the saddle girth tight enough and she and the saddle had slid clear around under the pony's stomach. "You'll get it right if you keep at it." And she had.

"Keep trying," she heard her father's voice saying. But her chairman wasn't a horse she could resaddle and mount until he accepted her as a teacher and poet. She could only smile at the image — he was really more like her first pony than a full grown horse, but still the image didn't work. To keep trying didn't have anything to do with him. She knew she could not convince him to keep her, could not convince him there was merit in her work. But "keep trying" was part of Anna's childhood, and now as an adult that necessity led her forward in spite of the depression, the heavy ache of fatigue that seemed to weight her every motion.

Anna slowed the car carefully and made a right turn onto the county road. It had been plowed and she relaxed her grip on the wheel and flexed her shoulders. She hated letting the memory of that encounter play again and again through her mind, but she didn't know how to avoid it. She took a deep breath. Focus on Wordsworth, she told herself, then angrily, fuck Wordsworth, fuck them all.

She was driving a road she had travelled to work every day, but today none of the landmarks worked for her. When she had first moved to these hills and mountains, Anna had felt at home, felt physically and emotionally comforted by the landscape. It was so different from the flat, monotonous beauty of the southwestern deserts and sagebrush of her home, that she could not really understand this affinity, from what source within herself it rose. Each day, as she drove this road, she had chosen a favorite curve in the road to notice a vista, said good morning to a delicate tall reaching elm that had resisted blight and chainsaws, marked the change of seasons by nuances of color tone in the elm's leaves and bark. But today, in her preoccupation, she had missed seeing the elm, and as she approached one of the most striking vistas, where the near hills opened out into the meadows and mountains beyond, a dog jumped awkwardly out of the deep snow and into the road directly in front of Anna's car. She swerved sharply to the left, caught the car as it began to fishtail, but couldn't stop the skid. She swung around sideways and skidded down into the ditch, landing with a crunch and a thud.

Anna sat clutching the steering wheel, her pulse racing. She took a deep breath and looked back toward the road. She hadn't hit the dog, at least. But Betsy was in a mess. Both right wheels had sunk deep into the ditch and the car hung at a precarious angle, not about to go anywhere under its own steam, not even with her help. So much for Wordsworth. Her watch told her the class started in fifteen minutes and not even if she got a lucky hitch would she be able to make her first class.

Anna climbed out of the car. She clambered through the snow, trying to see if Betsy's right side was crushed or just incapacitated, but the snow was too deep. As she waded back out to the road, a jeep came around the bend toward her. Anna laughed with relief. It was Chip, on his way to prune in the orchard. She leaned against Betsy, trying to look nonchalant, her arms crossed casually against her chest.

"Ahyeah," he reflected, walking around the car speculatively. "Couldn't you have dug it in any deeper?"

"Now, Chip," Anna remonstrated, "I did the best I could. I think that's quite respectably in the ditch."

Chip laughed assent, looked at her intently. "You O.K.?"

"Yeah," Anna admitted, "just shaken. And tired. Real tired."

"What happened?" Chip was serious now, concerned.

"Dog jumped out in front of me." Anna explained what she remembered of the accident. "I don't think I was quite all there," she admitted reluctantly.

"You want me to take you to school or back home?"

Anna looked up in surprise. "Home?"

"Sure. You just had an accident." He seemed exasperated at her question. "Can't you call in and say you can't get there?"

"God, what a wonderful idea, Chip." Why hadn't it occurred to her? "I feel better already. God. Yes. Take me home." The relief sweeping over her made her giddy.

"Come on then. I'll come back with the truck and tow the car over to the garage. I don't think it's much hurt."

Anna pulled her briefcase out of the front seat and climbed up into the high jeep. She felt she could let herself be taken care of by Chip, that this help came without demand. Headed back toward the orchard, she noticed the buds on the elm tree seemed to have swollen over the weekend and she was sure she could catch a hint of yellow at the tips of the high delicate branches where the snow had fallen off.

# Chapter 5

Anna stretched out comfortably in a chair in front of Elizabeth's fireplace and put her feet up on the coffee table, her wine glass on the table next to her under the dim lamp. She wiggled her toes in their woolly socks and sighed luxuriously. It had been a wonderful day — a gift really—and she had spent time writing in her journal about learning to take such days for herself instead of being forced into them by circumstance or exhaustion. She and Elizabeth had exchanged war stories over dinner with the children bouncing in and out — her auto accident and Elizabeth's recalcitrant goose—and Anna heard herself making light of what had happened, joking about how she must have known Chip was on his way with white horse and shining armour. But she didn't feel cheerful about it, she felt threatened, and she hoped now the children were in bed that she and Elizabeth might be able to talk about her fears, her sense that she was losing control of herself, her life, her direction, that she couldn't even make simple choices now, like deciding to read and prepare a poem for class, and make herself do what she had chosen.

When Chip had dropped her off at her house, she went into her study to work, but restlessness drove her outside and she split wood for an hour, letting her body find a physical exhaustion to match her mental and emotional depletion. She slept then, a deep and satisfying sleep without remembered dreams, and woke and read and had been able to write in her journal. Chip drove Betsy back in the late afternoon, her wheels realigned and her fender bent back into place, only missing a little more paint and some rust. It could have been worse, Chip agreed laconically, and she thanked him with a laugh and a bearhug.

Elizabeth came into the quiet room and stood on the hearth in front of the fireplace, silent for a moment. She felt exhausted, depleted. After a day with the children now, she didn't have her old resiliency, couldn't take a deep breath and go plunging on into something new. Was it age? Or having the fifth baby? He was an easy baby, she always reassured her friends who worried about how she would cope. But sometimes now she was beginning to realize that wasn't the point. Her energy was finite, not unlimited like she'd thought when she was twenty. She stooped down to the hay-lined box at the side of the hearth. The two downy-furred goslings started to cheep when they recognized her. She smiled and ran a finger over the top of each nearly bald head, settling the hay in around them. She stood again and sighed.

"That damned goose. You wouldn't believe how upset I was this morning." Elizabeth felt slightly chagrined to admit the extent of her feeling about the baby geese. Anna had, after all, been in an accident, what might have been a serious accident. She hoped her concern didn't seem ridiculous to Anna, but still she was not able to release it, stop talking about it to Anna.

"Yes, I would believe it. You're like that." Anna smiled up at her. "I mean, first of all your goose wouldn't be a good mother. I expect you would find that upsetting. And then you have to bring them indoors, sort out the dead ones, keep the cats and dogs from attacking the live ones. It's not as if that's all you had to do today, you know." She paused. "Have they imprinted on you? Are you their mother now?"

Elizabeth laughed. "Frankly," she confessed, "I was hoping they would imprint on Colin. He's about the right size and wouldn't mind them waddling around after him all day."

Both women laughed at her image and the room seemed warm and protected. Their voices were low and relaxed as they went on and recounted the rest of their day.

Elizabeth had been afraid of Anna when they first met, afraid of that professional part of her life that seemed so distant from the life Elizabeth led, so similar to the differences between her and Edward. She had married Edward the summer of her junior year in college and never returned to finish her degree. She knew herself to be intelligent, interested in ideas and theories, but more and more Edward treated her as though she could not understand the ideas he wanted to talk about, the issues he wanted to argue. Elizabeth hated his pompous friends and used her preoccupation with the children and the animals to separate herself from Edward's social life. She made herself tell Anna, "Well, I never graduated from college, you know."

"Why?" Anna asked, as if she might have had reasons.

Elizabeth recounted her boredom, the emptiness of sorority and fraternity life. Anna just nodded. It seemed reasonable to her and Elizabeth was relieved.

"In my family," Anna confessed, "a college degree is something we look at with suspicion." She half laughed. "When I wanted to go to school, they wouldn't let me go to the University of Oklahoma, that was too high-falutin'. I had to go to the State U. where I'd get more grounding." She groaned. "Just me and the ag-tech jocks in my English classes. You can imagine how happy I made my English teachers." She laughed fully with remembrance. "When I finally got out I'd had so much grounding I decided to apply to the most esoteric, ungrounded program I could find. That's how I got to England. Talk about culture shock."

And she told Elizbeth about the strangeness of being in that large, busy, dirty city, walking through the huge stone fortress walls into the Unversity, feeling always when she spoke that she was marked by her slow accent, by her very words and by her perspective, marked too by her body, how she moved and held herself and filled her space. She felt finally she had become acculturated in some degree when she learned to keep her elbows at her side when she walked, her knees together when she sat.

Elizabeth was not afraid of Anna now; she felt protective of her, knew that she was hurt, vulnerable at this point in her life. She wanted to reach out to her — how she was not sure — but she found herself wanting to touch Anna, to hug and hold her and heal her. But Anna's body language did not permit cuddling — she's not Shanna, after all, Elizabeth reminded herself when she felt these impulses — although Anna's boundaries had begun to relax in the few months Elizabeth had known her. Now the soft glow of the fire reflected in her wine glass and Elizabeth turned sideways in her chair to observe Anna's pensive profile.

"So how are you feeling?" she asked, sensing Anna's need to talk more.

To Anna's surprise, she felt tears start down her cheeks. She could not speak for a moment, then wiped her face with the back of her hand. "Not great, I guess," she admitted ruefully.

Elizabeth waited quietly.

"I guess I just feel lost," Anna's voice was nearly a whisper. "I can't figure out where I am. There's some part of me doing things I don't understand and I can't seem to control it." She turned to look at Elizabeth, to see if she had understood. The fire light had darkened Elizabeth's eyes, silvered her hair. She is a beautiful woman, Anna thought.

"Try and tell me more," said Elizabeth. "I think I know what you're saying. Is it like being in England was at first?"

Anna reflected. "Not exactly. In England I knew there were rules. As soon as I learned them, then when I did something, I got results I could count on." She paused. That sounded terribly convoluted. "Like when I walked into my tutor's office without my academic gown on and he thought I was just there for a social visit and wouldn't talk about my essay with me. When I put my gown on, he knew I was there for academic business."

Elizabeth nodded, "Right, if you can read the map, you'll get there eventually."

Anna agreed, "But now. . . " She sighed and shrugged. Now what, she wondered. What in the world was wrong with her? "Now, I guess I feel like I'm in terriory that hasn't been mapped. For me, anyway. I have all these strange feelings, strange dreams," she paused, but did not elaborate. "When I was in college I took a Phys. Ed. course in how to teach swimming to blind children." She tried to think how this was relevant to what she was saying. "They were incredible. If you told them there was water and you would be there to catch them, they'd just jump right off the edge. I couldn't imagine having that much faith in what anybody told me."

"Me either," said Elizabeth. "I'd have to find out what was there for myself."

"But one exercise we did — it was to show them how to do a front crawl stroke, when they couldn't see it, you know — so we held up a towel and showed them the motions of climbing the towel like it was a rope, hand over hand. So they could imagine what the crawl stroke was like in the water. And it worked. They learned to do it."

"That's amazing," Elizabeth agreed, but her voice was tentative, she did not quite understand what Anna meant.

"I guess I feel like I'm in the dark. Floating around making aimless motions. And I want someone to hold up a towel for me and show me how to get control again." She turned in her chair and pulled her knees up, wrapping her arms around them and resting her chin.

"Do you think it's all about your job?" Elizabeth asked after a moment.

"No," Anna looked directly at her, then away. "I know it's about more than my job." She was silent, confused. How had Elizabeth gone so directly to the point, what could she have seen, Anna wondered. Were all of her feelings so visible to others when she was only beginning to see them for herself? And what could she share of this confusion, when she didn't know if her feelings were real, if they would last, or if they were a temporary response? She could hardly say she hated all men. That was what she felt much of the time, and yet it wasn't true as long as Chip was her friend. Perhaps it was that she was angry at her chairman and her colleagues in the department who seemed so false now, so full of their own egos they couldn't see beyond themselves, their small petty jealousies and favoritisms.

Anna could feel Elizabeth waiting for her to say something further. She stretched in her chair, then got up and went to stand by the hearth. The goslings ignored her, even when she bent down close to them, bringing her face within inches of their tiny downy bodies. She could see each pin feather barely covering the vulnerable grey-white skin with fluff.

She stood and stretched again and looked over to Elizabeth who was gazing into the fire. Anna drew in her breath sharply and thought, how can I say, women attract me? You, Elizabeth, with your strong, compact body, your rough calloused hands, the soft curve of you small breasts, I am attracted to you, I want to hold you and feel the softness of your cheek against mine. It seemed such a step, a commitment, to admit such a thing – like the intelligent faith of those blind children, stepping off into they knew not what, but knowing they could never go back without encountering what was beneath them. At one level, Anna knew, she found the potential encounter thrilling, energizing, the most exciting possibliity in her life; at another level, it terrified her. Now she breathed again, deeply, trying to calm her pulse and create a casual voice.

"Did I tell you about the most recent meeting with the Women's Coalition students?"

"No. You just said you'd gotten a mysterious message that they had to see you and it was urgent."

"Well, it was important, I think. About eight of them came trooping in. It was an internal disagreement — at least that's what they told me at first. Some of them wanted men to join the Women's Coalition and the rest were furious. Said women needed their own space, needed to do some things on their own." Anna leaned forward in her chair, concentrated on her memory of the conflict. "I could tell they were upset, but I didn't think—for some reason — they were telling me the whole story."

"Were they?"

"No. I finally asked Lee — she's one of my thesis students — what the real problem was. She evaded it for a while, but finally admitted that it's going around campus that everyone involved in the Coalition is a lesbian." Anna paused as she said the word aloud, then smiled.

"Really," she told Elizabeth, "it was like watching the chorus in a Greek tragedy when Lee said the word. You should have seen the looks on their faces."

She had, herself, felt deep shock at hearing the word spoken aloud. Later she realized she had probably not heard the word more than once or twice in her life, however often she might have read or thought of it, and speaking it aloud semed to give it a larger life.

"Some of the students thought that if they invited men to their meetings, it would make it seem less like they were lesbians," Anna continued, making herself use the word to Elizabeth, her tone casual in that warm, comfortable space.

"Well, I guess it might," Elizabeth nodded. "What did you tell them they should do?"

"Not much," Anna admitted. "They can hardly put out an announcement that they aren't lesbians. I mean, I think some of them are." She looked over to see whether Elizabeth would react to this, but her face seemed only mildly curious.

"I didn't know what to tell them." She had felt her own insecurity surface as she looked down into their anxious frowning faces. I wonder if they've said that about me? Is that what Frank thinks? "Finally I just told them to wait it out, that something more interesting would come along pretty soon for the campus to gossip about. That seemed to satisfy them." She shrugged. "I hope it works."

"Do you think they are? Lesbians?"

Anna nodded. "They told me so. It was the last thing Lee said as they filed out. She turned back and said, 'Some of us *are* lesbian.' She really stressed it."

"What did you say?"

Anna laughed. "What could I say? I just nodded astutely and said, 'yes.' I mean what does one say to something like that?" Elizabeth was shaking her head agreeing. What does one say, Anna repeated to herself again, and the room was silent.

After a moment, Elizabeth reached over to the table and poured the rest of the nearly empty wine bottle into their glasses.

"Well, I think it was brave of her to say it." Elizabeth turned her glass and stared at it thoughtfully, not looking at Anna. She felt moved by the evening, moved by Anna's willingness to talk so much with her — she felt vital after these conversations, as though all of her best resources had been used, had been made available to her and to Anna — and she wished she had some way to thank Anna. Anna would probably not understand why she was being thanked, Elizabeth argued with herself, she'd never know why conversations like this are such a relief. She was staring at the fire when suddenly she saw one of the dogs, lying in her line of vision, flicker an ear, then raise his head. Her attention wavered and she cocked her head, too. She heard a car coming. Who would be driving up the road at this time of night, she was wondering as the car pulled into her driveway and the dogs headed eagerly toward the door. Tom. Oh, god, she had forgotten that Tom might come back tonight. She looked quickly at Anna, who seemed not to have noticed the car.

"I think Tom just drove in," she said casually.

"He did?" Anna was perplexed, her forehead wrinkled. "I thought he was out on the road?"

Elizabeth shrugged. "He must have finished early. He'll take off again in the morning." As she heard his steps on the porch, she added almost defensively, "He likes to sleep home when he can."

The two women sat quietly waiting for Tom to come into the room. He was loud, boisterous, and drunk, they both realized at once.

"Hello, girls," he said cheerfully, leaning down to give Elizabeth a kiss. He stayed bent over her for a moment, swaying slightly. "Well," he announced, "I couldn't find any warm beds down in Bennington, so I thought I'd come home."

Anna recognized her exit line and sat forward in her chair. "I guess I'll be heading home."

"No," Tom held out a hand. "You all have to keep me company for another drink. After all," he picked up the empty wine bottle and waved it toward them, "I've got to have a chance to catch up with you." He wandered into the kitchen.

Anna could not look at Elizabeth. She sat forward, quiet, furious, thinking, this is why I can't stand men, thank god I don't have to go to bed with him, I wish he were anywhere in the world now but in the next room, between me and Elizabeth. When he came back into the living room, Anna stood and looked directly at him. His heavy dark beard stubbled his cheeks and made him look swarthy, contrasting with the red lines in his nose and high cheekbones.

"Sorry not to stay, Tom, but I've got an early morning."

He nodded and sank down into a chair.

"I'll walk you out, Anna," Elizabeth said. She was glad Tom had come home, but sorry they had lost the mood of a moment before. She still wanted to say something to Anna, but couldn't think of anything as she stood and watched her pull on a down vest and stuff gloves in her pocket. She opened the door and stepped out in the cold night air with Anna. Impulsively, she took Anna's arm and pulled her around into an embrace.

"Thank you," she said, "thank you for coming over tonight."

She was only a few inches shorter than Anna, Elizabeth realized, standing with her hands on the other woman's shoulders. She reached up and kissed Anna's lips, pressed her cheek to Anna's cheek for a moment, whispered, "good night," then turned and went back into the house.

Anna felt Elizabeth's warm breath saying thank you, felt her lips pressed, felt the soft cheek next to her own. She stood speechless as Elizabeth said goodnight and went into the house, closing the door gently behind her. She walked out into the night, parting the crisp air before her, slicing it with her exhilaration. Soft, her cheek was soft. She had never seen the stars so stunningly bright. The milky way cut a swathe through the ebony black sky, making its name seem appropriate to her for the first time. Joy, thought Anna as she leaned against her car for a moment looking up into the crystal night. Joy.

# Chapter 6
## March

"Have you never just stopped writing poems?" Clair set the teapot down in the center of the table and arranged the cozy around it.

"No," Anna said, reflecting for a moment. "I think this is the closest I've ever come to feeling I couldn't write. Usually my writing helps me through the difficult times. Does your painting work that way for you?"

Clair shook her head. It never had, she realized. She wondered how much she could say, as she looked across the table at Anna's open, serious face.

"No," she said finally, "my painting takes me to the hard places, it doesn't get me through them. It takes me — I don't know — but when I paint seriously, I'm usually terrified." She smiled at Anna, then shrugged, dismissing her fear.

"What kind of places do you mean?" Anna asked, unwilling to change the mood of their conversation.

"Empty places," Clair said abruptly, then pushed away from the table and went to the large hanging cupboard and brought out two ceramic mugs. She stood with her back to the cupboard, facing Anna, the cups clutched against her stomach.

"Here." She gestured with the cups. "I feel empty at my center when I paint." She felt nervous at the admission, but willing to see how Anna responded.

"Have you ever gone on when that happens? Pushed through it, I mean, to see what it was about?"

"No." Clair was surprised at the question. She poured the tea, then said quietly, "It never seemed to me that it could mean anything but emptiness, barrenness—you know, no resources." Enough of me, she thought, asking, "Hasn't it ever happened to you? Do you know what I'm talking about?"

"Maybe." Anna could see Clair's anxiety, could sense that the conversaton was pushing their newly established intimacy. Excitement shoved her forward on the edge of her chair, both elbows resting on the kitchen table, as she tried to find a way to speak to the intelligence she could see hovering behind the fear in Clair's soft brown eyes. She tried to speak carefully.

"Maybe. Sometimes when I find a place that seems empty it just feels that way because it's unfamiliar." Clair was frowning into her tea mug, masking her eyes. Anna searched her experience for an example. "Like when my mother died."

Clair looked up, expectant. "Did you write poems about that?"

"I tried at first. But I felt that her death had left an empty place in me. That whenever I tried to think about her or write about her, all I felt was that empty place." Anna was speaking rapidly now, searching in her mind for the words to illustrate this new realization. "What I was really finding, of course, was all the things you'd expect – grief, anger that she had left me, love that didn't have anyplace to go – but I couldn't recognize the feelings. Because whenever I had cried before she'd always been there to comfort me. Learning grief without her was like being in a room I should have known, but couldn't recognize. Maybe it felt empty." Anna stopped speaking abruptly. She looked at Clair and smiled. "Does that make any sense? Does it sound like anything you were talking about?"

"I don't know," Clair admitted, trying to sound casual, "but it does make me think I might go back and check out some of those empty places and see if they were really as bad as they seemed."

Anna grinned. "Good."

Clair smiled back at her. "You think that sense of emptiness might just be the entrance to something new? Like standing at the mouth of a cave – or one of those ancient labyrinths – it looks like gaping emptiness, but there really are things to find in there if you keep groping around?"

"I think so. For me, anyway, that's been how it seems to work. How it feels."

Their talk drifted to other things, rested a while in details of where Clair could buy her paints up-country, not at the local store, surely, they laughed, unless she wanted to do a mural in house paint on the side of the barn. Anna kept another realization close to her. She came to Clair's hoping she could talk with her about Elizabeth, hint somehow about her feelings, test Clair's response before she risked more with Elizabeth. But she could not seem to introduce the subject and now, as she sat having tea with Clair on this foggy March afternoon, she only hoped Elizabeth would stop by the kitchen when she finished her work up at the evaporator.

Clair had watched Anna falling in love with Elizabeth. She was not surprised when she first thought it. The two were similar in a way Clair recognized, but could not define. A certain physicality was all she could call it, although the term was inadequate for what she felt in the presence of each of them. She admitted that her feelings were confused – some of them – too close to the surface, threatening. She was, in the first place, jealous. She counted on Elizabeth for some sense of intimacy in her life. Although she could not say that had changed – in spite of Paul, she and Elizabeth were still together every day and talked at the same personal level – nonetheless, she sensed that Elizabeth and Anna shared things that did not come back to her, and she was fearful of losing Elizabeth. She wanted to know Anna better, but felt that Anna might be so caught up in Elizabeth she would not have time for her – this she felt in spite of the obvious pleasure Anna seemed to have in their talk about art.

Clair saw Anna walk over to the window and look casually up at the barn, watching for Elizabeth to start down to the kitchen. She wondered if the friendship had "gone further," wondered if they were lovers now. For she noticed that they seemed more restrained in the last few days in their physical expressions of affection toward one another. When they greeted one another now in front of her, there was a studied casualness, a restraint that only heightened the attraction she felt between them.

As Anna walked back to the table, Clair watched her speculatively. Anna was thirty-one, attractive, intelligent; she would surely fall in love with a man when she got out of this closed, trapped situation, Clair felt, surely find a man wherever her next job took her. This thought pleased her, the sense of Anna leaving and Clair and Elizabeth being together in this village again.

"Didn't you ever want children?" she asked Anna abruptly.

Anna looked surprised. "Actually, I did. I mean, I do. Why?"

Clair shrugged. Why? "Well, you're not getting any younger." She laughed at the cliche. "What I mean is that you probably ought to have them in the next couple of years and I just wondered if you'd thought about it, how you felt about children." She couldn't say, now that you've fallen in love with a woman, how are you going to have children of your own? "I wondered if you felt you had to make a choice between children and your poetry?"

"Sure, I've thought about that. We even talked about it in my Women Writers course in January. You know, the old thing about how women create in the womb and men create in their heads. I was amazed at how that old stereotype still hangs on." She combed her fingers through the length of her long, loose-hanging brown hair. "I mean, did you ever feel that because you'd had children you didn't have to paint any more, that everything in you was satisfied by that physical act?"

"Wait a minute," Clair said, forcibly pushing away from the table. "I asked you this question."

Anna was surprised at this defensive posture, but grinned good-naturedly, penitently. "Sorry. I forgot it was my turn." What had upset Clair? "Teaching full time. . . supporting myself, however I do it. . . " Anna didn't know what else to say. It was a conversation she could not have without pretending to assume there was man in her future and she was not making that assumption now. She felt unable to speak, resentful of this limitation, but she could not see her way around it.

"I guess if you want children you just have to have them at some point and other things get pushed around or adjusted." She paused, then conceded. "I do love children. And I think I'd like to be pregnant, have that physical experience. But some part of me doubts I'll ever have children." She paused again, shrugged.

Anna walked over to the stove and put more water in the tea kettle, then looked out the window again.

"Uh, oh," she said, turning to Clair, "speaking of which, here comes Colin."

She watched the stocky three year old make his way carefully down from the barn, his face set in serious concentration as he lifted his awkward snowmobile boots through the snow and mud. His straight bowl-cut blonde hair framed his face; Anna thought she could see something of Elizabeth in the way the child tossed his head to clear the hair from his face, not noticing that it settled back exactly where it had been.

"Mom says to tell you she's nearly done and we're freezin' to death," he announced importantly, pushing open the kitchen door. "And that I can have a cookie," he added, tentatively, not sure if this was his mother's kitchen or Clair's.

"Really!" Clair laughed and held him steady while he worked off the heavy boots and then unzipped his jacket. She went to the cookie jar on the kitchen counter. "Do you want hot chocolate, too, Colin?"

"Yes." He climbed up on a chair and rested his arms, chin, and shoulders on the table, completely at ease, Anna realized as she watched him. I wonder where he gets that self-assurance, why he assumes he will be welcome wherever he goes? For Colin had entered her own kitchen with that self-possessed right-to-be-here attitude.

And then Elizabeth pushed open the door, flung her hair away from her eyes with the same gesture Colin had used, caught Anna's glance instantly, and crinkled her eyes in a quick hello and turned to Clair.

"God, it's cold up in that barn. Damp clear through now with thaw. How can you let that husband of yours spend so many hours up there?" She held her red, chapped hands up to Clair's cheeks for a moment, then turned toward the stove.

"I hardly force him out of the house," Clair said, half laughing, half irritated at Elizabeth's presumption. But Elizabeth had meant nothing by it, Anna saw; she had already turned toward the stove, checked to see if the tea kettle was boiling, then lifted the lid off of a soup pot that had been simmering on the back of the stove since noon. She sniffed appreciatively, noted the contents, then replaced the lid. There was no possessiveness in the gesture and no judgment. She did not want the soup, nor think ill of it; she had merely wanted to know what was there. Anna thought Elizabeth was like that about so many things, matter of fact and accepting. In a flash, Anna saw that Elizabeth would be lifting the pot lids off of her children's lives for years to come, glancing in to see what was there, nonjudgmental, stirring around perhaps, making a carrot more visible here, a potato there, and then she would put the lid back on, satisfied, and they would resume their lives and privacy.

For a few moments the three women sat, chatting quietly, talking of soup and fireplaces and spring thaw, Colin dozing on his mother's lap.

"Guess what Clair's summer project is going to be," Anna said to Elizabeth, avoiding Clair's surprised look for a moment.

"Umm, strawberry preserves?" Elizabeth guessed.

"No," Anna drawled, now turning a laughing, teasing face toward Clair. "We've decided she's going to paint a mural on the far side of the barn, the side facing down toward the village, not cows or anything bucolic, something shocking," she was urging Clair now, "something they've never even imagined."

"That won't be too hard," Elizabeth insisted. "Most anything would shock us locals."

"Huh," Anna raised one eyebrow in disbelief. "I doubt it." Then she turned to Clair, "How about something feminist, something with women in it, being victorious and all that. We could call it Woman Rampant."

"How about woman rampaging," Elizabeth interrupted, "you could do a visual of Anna after she lost her job."

They all laughed and Clair agreed, "I'll think about it, I'll think about it," then added, "but do let me think about starting smaller than on the side of the barn. I've got a canvas stretched, sitting in the closet," she admitted. "I may just start with that."

Elizabeth looked at her in surprise and started to ask Clair, "When did you. . ." as Paul opened the door to the kitchen, stamped his muddy boots once on the porch, and then stepped inside the door.

"Whew," his face was red. He leaned down to take off his boots, pushing them carefully from the top to avoid the mud caked on the soles and half way up the boot. The women were silent, watching him. Now we are four, thought Anna, wondering if Paul could feel the hostility in their silence. As if in answer to her thought, Clair went to the stove to get him a cup of tea, and Elizabeth started to speak, her voice a little rushed and nervous.

"Why did you stay up there so long, you look absolutely frozen, come over here and sit down."

Paul obeyed, sitting heavily in one of the chairs next to Anna, looking over at Elizabeth. He looked tired, Anna thought, as he settled next to her. His shoulders drooped in a kind of weariness she had not seen in him before.

"Lots of interrupted nights?" she asked in a kind voice, overcompensating for her sense of his intrusion.

Elizabeth answered for him, "Lots of nights with nearly no sleep. We've been meeting one another coming and going at the evaporator. When the temperature goes up and down like this, it's hard to keep the fire steady." Her voice was strained, Anna thought, not listening to Paul's response, and she felt a tension in the kitchen she could not explain. Clair sat quietly at the end of the table.

When Paul and Elizabeth paused in their conversation about the sugaring, Anna rose from her chair. "Guess I'll get back to my desk."

Elizabeth looked at her watch. "Oh, shit, the school bus will be dropping the kids off any minute. I've got to get back, too." She went into the living room where Artie was sleeping on the sofa. "Get your boots on, Colin," her voice called from the other room.

Clair stood by the stove and watched the two women walk out the driveway towards their cars. They walked side by side; talking or silent, she could not tell from their backs. At the cars, Elizabeth turned and put Artie in the carrier chair and helped Colin climb into the front seat. Anna waited. When the children were settled, Elizabeth turned — it was like watching a silent movie, Clair thought — and took both of Anna's hands in hers, leaned forward unhurriedly and kissed her firmly on the mouth. Then they spoke briefly — she could see that — Anna smiled, their hands dropped and each woman turned toward her own car.

Behind her, Clair heard Paul's chair scrape out from the table. "I think I'll go upstairs and rest before milking," he said and she heard him go heavily up the stairs to the bedroom.

Alone now in the kitchen, Clair took her teacup back to the kitchen table. She sat at the table, washed by loneliness. She knew — and did not know—the source of her feeling. Paul, her husband for eighteen years, was upstairs sleeping in their bed. In a few moments, the school bus would pull up at the end of the driveway and Tammie and Sharon would tear into the kitchen, hungry, probably arguing. She had a lovely home, friends, she did the catalog again as she had so often in the past — all the things that were meant to satisfy, the conditions of her life for which she should be grateful. And she was not. Her hands clasping the tea mug were white at the knuckles, strain showed in the stillness of her attitude, a posture she held as if pushing against resistance, sitting quietly as she was, trying to understand the source of the anguish washing over her.

All right, she told herself, run it through and see what it is. She had learned to read herself like a litmus paper, separating each source of anxiety, naming it and checking her response. Children, she named first, their arrival so imminent, pushing them forward. That was easy. Clair felt her pulse trip, then accelerate, diffusing blood into her face. Children. The conversation with Anna about children. Had that been it? What had they said? She closed her eyes, trying to focus on the kitchen as it was an hour ago when she and Anna had sat talking. Something about Anna not having time for writing and children, wasn't that it? And then the other words floated back to her — did having children satisfy you? Make you feel you didn't have to paint?

Clair could not remember her answer now, but she allowed the question to sit for a moment on the surface of her consciousness, making an effort to buoy it up, keep it visible, not letting it sink, one edge first, then the other like an abandoned dory until it disappeared, waterlogged, from view. She wasn't sure the two questions, children and painting, were connected for her. Children, satisfied? It was not that she had never asked herself this question before, but that her conversation with Anna had jolted the question into a new dimension. Anna wanted children, but was probably not going to have them. Clair had never wanted children, and here she was trying to mother two of them.

Trying. She heard the squeal of the school bus brakes, a pause and then the surge of the engine as it pulled away. She watched her children come up the driveway toward her. Tammie was ten-year-old exuberant, leaping over some puddles in the pot-holed driveway, splashing through others, swinging her book satchel through the damp spring air. Behind her plodded Sharon, tall, heavy-featured, glum.

For a moment Clair had a glimpse of herself as a child — I was like both of them, she realized — both of them in one body. She remembered days when she had thought her life was the best, the only possible; the shabby two room apartment she shared with her mother was a castle in a busy kingdom. On those days, she had played for hours up and down the corridors, alone or with a friend, tormenting the elderly neighbors, hiding in the back stairwell, marking out territory, repelling invaders. But on other days, the stale air of the apartment and the corridors had settled a heavy mantle over her head and shoulders, leaving her no air, no movement, no escape from the continuous intimacy she shared with her mother. But was it just age, she wondered, looking again at her two children? She thought not, but could not remember; each picture of those heavy days she tried to conjure slid away before she could focus on it.

"Hi, Mom," Tammie burst into the kitchen. "Whatsta eat?"

"Anything in the icebox," Clair said, turning toward her. "What's wrong with Sharon, Tammie? Did something happen in school today?"

Tammie pulled her head out of the refrigerator to give Clair a surprised look, then shrugged and went back in. "I don't know. She's mad, I think. But I don't know what." She tucked her booty in one arm, picked up her satchel and headed for the stairs to her room.

Clair took the lid off the soup pot and started to stir it. She wanted to be doing something when Sharon came in. She paused, waited for the door, then stirred again.

"Hi, hon," she said casually, turning toward her daughter. Sharon did not reply.

"How was your day?" Clair could see Sharon's mouth turned down at the corners, just like Paul's when he was angry. "What's wrong, Sharon? Did something happen at school today?"

"Oh, Mom," Sharon's voice was resentful. "Don't you ever remember anything I tell you?" She slammed her book satchel on the kitchen table and sat down to take off her boots.

Clair searched her memory, trying to find a clue to Sharon's anger. Had she told her something this morning?

"I didn't get elected yearbook editor." Sharon's voice burst out angrily, interrupting Clair's search. Oh, god, she remembered, yes, that was it. Today were the senior class yearbook elections.

"Oh, honey, I'm so sorry." Clair went over and stood by Sharon, her hand reaching tentatively toward her shoulder, but not able to touch it, so tense was her daughter's body.

"You *are* not sorry." Sharon stood and turned and faced Clair angrily. "you are *not* sorry." She was shouting now, her face red and teary.

Clair started to protest, but Sharon interrupted her. "You're not sorry at all or you never would have made me move up here. I know I would have been elected editor in New Jersey. All my friends were there. People knew me. These stupid kids don't even know me." Her voice was rising shrilly as she finished. "You've ruined my high school years." Hurling this final indictment, she turned and stomped up the stairs.

Clair stood and listened until she heard Sharon's bedroom door slam. She shook her head, clearing her thoughts for a moment. Where did she get that? Ruined my high school years. As if they were something particular, separate from all of her other years.

She walked over to the window where she had been standing when the school bus drove up. She had been thinking about something important; she stood by the partly open window trying to remember what it was, but the surface of her mind had closed over the thought, sending it back down the labyrinth of years. She stared out at the mud and slush held on the surface of the still frozen earth. Most of the snow had melted off of the hill behind the barn, leaving only a ridge of grey ice along the northern crest where the sun came last and left first. March was such an unpleasant month, she thought, even the air smelled like moldy time. Turning back into the kitchen, she felt a depression settle down over her again. She had never liked March. She'd feel better when the real spring came.

# Chapter 7

Elizabeth drove up the long driveway, past the darkened house and into the barnyard. Her body, heavy with the fatigue of a dozen nights of interrupted sleep, responded slowly, almost autonomously to the necessity of climbing out of the car, trudging through hardening slush up to the open barn doors. They had set the evaporator up just inside the open doors on the hard earth floor, hoping to hold some of the heat from the fire in the barn while letting the water vapor escape out into the air. She paused before she entered the barn, enjoying as always the dark glow of the fire flickering under the evaporator, reflecting in quick flashes off the tools stored in the back of the barn, off the low hanging eaves of the hay mow, the hinges of animal pens along one side. The usual smells of the barn—animals, hay, the sharp acrid tinge of silage – had an exotic, almost tropical sweetness of moist maple. Elizabeth breathed deeply. In the corner pen a young doe goat heard her and baaed insistently.

"Hi, Jenny," Elizabeth walked over to the pen and scratched the doe's soft ears. She enjoyed the midnight solitude, the sense of herself awake and alone while the whole world slept around her.

Turning back toward the evaporator, she hoped Paul would not come down to her tonight, hoped he would be too tired, would not have heard her car come up the drive. She lifted the large heavy logs, taking them one or two at time over to the door of the rough-rigged wood stove. When she was ready to load, she opened the door and the fire whooshed dramatically, fed by the cold night air. Quickly she shoved in one log, then another, pushing each farther to the back of the long barrel-length stove, deliberate, yet hurrying so that the added heat wouldn't collect and make the evaporator boil over. Finally she shut the door firmly and stood, her face heated with exertion and the flames of the fire. She waited by the stove for a moment, letting her eyes adjust to the dark again, then checked the level of the evaporator. It was still high. She wouldn't have to add more sap tonight, she decided. Good. She was done. And Paul had not come down.

She paused for a moment, then went over and stood by Jenny's pen and rubbed her ears again affectionately. In the silence of the night she heard the kitchen door open and close softly. Paul was coming. You can get in the car and drive home now, she told herself. And yet she stood, rooted, next to the pen, half hidden in the shadow, a thrilling and disturbing tension building in her lower legs, mounting, spreading, filling her whole body.

He had come down that first night of this long run, and when Elizabeth had heard him clear his throat as he walked up to the barn, she had been angry, greeting him hostilely and assuming he was checking on her now because she had done something wrong on one of the nights during the first run. He had cleared his throat again, almost nervously, not greeting her, walking silently into the barn.

"Is something wrong?" Elizabeth asked, cold and distant.

"No." He seemed surprised. It had never occurred to him that she would not welcome his presence.

Elizabeth did not believe him, but went on with her work as though he were not there. She lifted the five gallon pail off a hook, filled it with sap and carried it to the evaporator, not looking at him, hoping he would not offer to help. He didn't.

"I just couldn't sleep," he said, after her silence.

Elizabeth did not answer. She glanced at him, hung the bucket back up by the collection tank and turned to leave the barn.

She was not surprised when he came again the second night.

"Sometimes," he began the conversation as though twenty-four hours had not elapsed, "sometimes I just get lonely." He paused and looked to see if she had heard him. Elizabeth went on carrying the logs. "I guess," he was tentative, trying again, "there just aren't many sensitive people around here I feel I can talk to."

"Your wife is sensitive," Elizabeth said sharply, but she was moved enough by his apparent vulnerability to add, more softly, "but I can see it might be hard."

Driving home that night she reflected that she had never thought that a man might be lonely. Most of the women she knew were lonely, it seemed inevitable, the way women's lives were arranged. But she never thought of men as having the same sense of isolation, of drifting in empty, undefined space. The men she knew — Tom, Edward, her father and brothers — were all too busy, too directed out at the world to ever seem lonely to her. It was she who needed them, used ploys to bring their attention back to her, make them notice her and stay with her a while before they went back into their own worlds. But Paul had said he was lonely. She pondered. Did that make him special, different from other men?

On the third night she turned and confronted him, "So why are you lonely?" she asked, and he relaxed at her question, feeling now that she was engaged in this interaction. He knew he had established the first foot hold.

He shrugged in the fire's twilight. "I don't know. It's solitary, this life. In New Jersey I never worked alone — always someone at the next desk, in a meeting. . . "

"You mean having people around kept you from being lonely? That's stupid." She was deliberately belligerent. "You can't believe that."

Taken aback at her directness, Paul felt his defenses start to reassert themselves. He walked away from the fire for a moment, stood under the open sky looking at the bright stars. This wasn't what he wanted. He walked back into the barn, stood very close to Elizabeth and said softly, "You're right. It was just that having a lot of people around kept me busy in a different kind of way. You know, there's less time to think, to feel things."

He squatted now next to the fire and crossed his hands around his knees. "And of course I had Clair down there, at first." He paused.

Elizabeth felt her scalp tingle. She knew, and did not want to know, what he meant. She wanted to hear and did not want to hear what he was going to say next. "You have Clair now," she heard herself say and she got in the car to drive home.

He came around to her side of the car. "You know what I mean," he insisted.

Elizabeth could not sleep when she climbed back into her bed that night, woke tired and distressed to the alarm the next morning, irritated with the children, barely able to get through the routine of getting them ready for the school bus. She felt as though there was something she ought to be doing about Paul's pending confidences, but she could not imagine what it was. She could hardly go to Clair and ask her to keep Paul in bed when Elizabeth's car drove up. She couldn't stop going, although it was ridiculous, she told herself, for both of them to be up in the middle of the night. They were meant to trade shifts, Paul stoking the fire when he went to bed at ten o'clock, Elizabeth coming in at one, Paul again at four and Elizabeth starting the day after the school bus had left. But she wanted the money from the sale of the syrup; she wanted the money desperately. The anticipation of some income from her own labor was immediate and necessary to her sense of independence and self reliance. And she could not claim the money if she did not do her fair share of the work. She couldn't say to Paul, well, if you're having insomnia, how about stoking up for me? And, finally, she had to admit that she wanted to know. She was curious, curious with a heightened excitement that would not let her turn aside from this revelation. She did not see how it could affect Clair. Nothing, she promised herself, could ever change her feelings about Clair.

He was walking up the driveway as she pulled into the barnyard. "Look," he began, his voice apologetic, "I didn't mean to upset you last night. It's just that you're Clair's friend."

He didn't continue and Elizabeth said nothing, but went toward the woodpile. He walked beside her and lifted the logs with her. Together, they stoked the stove.

When she went to check the evaporator level, he said, "It's O.K., I think." Elizabeth thought to herself, he's been out here before. He's probably been out here all night. She wished he would hurry up and say it.

"Well, I guess that's it for tonight," she said. "Wait a minute, O.K.?" Paul put his hand on her arm. "Look, you're Clair's friend," he said again. "She must have told you about her breakdown, hasn't she?"

Elizabeth said nothing, shrugged. Clair had, by innuendo. But she had never called it a breakdown.

He took her shrug for affirmation. "Well, you must have noticed. . . well, that you have to be a little careful around Clair."

Elizabeth was surprised, and her surprise camouflaged for a moment the open snare she had seen lying so clearly on the ground between them.

"What do you mean, careful?" Her question moved her forward and she did not at first feel the tightening, did not understand that her own motion now would inevitably secure her in the trap.

"You can't say things that upset her. She gets nervous and depressed so easily." His voice became husky, "That's what I mean about lonely. I just can't share everything with her any more. She's too fragile." Elizabeth was moved by the sound of tears in his voice, moved away from her own immediate response, which was that she had never held back or been "careful" with Clair.

"Tell me what happened in New Jersey," she said now, her voice warm and sympathetic. Might as well hear it all. Might as well get it over with.

And she listened with a careful ear, hearing the story now from Paul, noting the small differences at first. Finally as the story unfolded, she felt that the two versions had almost nothing in common except the beginning and end: we lived in New Jersey, now we live here.

What should she believe? Was it possible that Clair had been as Paul described, unable to keep house, unwilling to care for her children, that he came home one day and found her crying hysterically for no reason that anyone, not even Clair herself, could discern? He hadn't wanted to hospitalize her, he insisted, but there was no other remedy. He must think of the children, after all, and they were so upset.

"She just lost it completely," he said. "She didn't know who we were or where she was." And so he called the hospital. "It was what she wanted. I asked her and she said, yes, I should call them. I never wanted to hurt her," he said.

And then the doctors recommended quiet. They both felt that their life in New Jersey was too hectic. He had always wanted to farm—Elizabeth had heard this part of the story before — and so they took all of their savings, sold their suburban house and here they were. But he had to be careful. She was better, but he could never relax and be sure of her.

The night was a cold one, crystal clear again, all the radiant heat of the day's sun drained back off into the vast darkness. Elizabeth felt numb. Her toes and fingers ached with the cold and something inside her ached, too. She had to ask him, she decided. She couldn't go home tonight without asking.

She drew a deep breath. "What about the trouble in your. . . your brokerage house?"

He just looked at her, his head to one side. His shadow in the glow of the fire loomed behind them on the barn floor. "What do you mean?"

"What about the indictment and the missing funds?"

"Jesus Christ," he exploded, his body rigid with anger, then lowered his voice. "Did she tell you that? How many other people has she told? Do you see what I have to live with?" he turned toward her, his voice accusing now. "Do you see?"

Elizabeth stepped back, defensive. "No, I don't see." She was belligerent, mirroring his posture and attitude.

"She made that up." His voice was low and urgent. "Don't you see? That was part of her breakdown. I don't know where she got it from, but it's how she explains to herself what happened. But, Jesus," he exhaled, bringing his hand to his head in a gesture of pain, "here I am trying to run a farm, a business that depends 90% on getting credit, and my wife is telling people I'm a thief." His voice was close to breaking now, and his shadow diminished as his head and shoulder lowered.

After a moment, he raised his head and looked directly at Elizabeth. "Did you believe that of me?" he asked.

"I never thought about it," she said after a moment. "It wasn't something to believe or not. It just came up." She was confused. She wanted to be alone, have a chance to think about what Paul had said. She didn't know what to think or feel and she did not know what she should say to Paul now. Did she believe it? Did it matter, whether it had happened or not? She did not know. Masking her confusion, she turned to go, but first said, "You don't have to worry. I'm sure Clair hasn't told anyone else."

When she pulled in the driveway the next morning, Elizabeth went straight up to the barn. Usually she stopped at the house first and left off Colin and Artie in the warm kitchen. But this morning was unusually balmy, she told herself, even though the sun had not yet come over the hill. She left Artie sucking his thumb and dozing in the car seat, while Colin followed her around the barn, happily dogging her steps, asking questions and getting in the way. By the time she finished, the sun was well over the hill and Elizabeth was tired, hungry, and looking forward to coffee and a second breakfast with Clair. She could hear the milking machine still running in the next barn and knew she would have some time alone with Clair before Paul came in.

"Why didn't you leave the kids off this morning?" Clair asked as Elizabeth opened the kitchen door. "I was worried something was wrong."

"I was helping with the collectin'," Colin announced proudly.

"You were?" Clair was impressed and generous. She looked up at Elizabeth, a question still in her eyes.

Elizabeth shrugged. "It seemed like a mild morning, so I just took them up with me." She paused, thinking of Paul's warning and her chest tightened. "Besides, I never asked you if you minded keeping my kids. I've just been dumping them off here on you."

She looked at Clair, worry bringing her jaw line taut. What if Paul was right? What if Clair really didn't want children, didn't want to have to take care of them?

Clair's voice was dry and tinged with irony. "Don't you think you'd have known by now, if I minded keeping them?"

"Of course." Elizabeth laughed, relieved for a moment. "Of course I would. What's for breakfast?"

Elizabeth drove home to her own chores, thinking to herself that she could be Clair's friend and Paul's friend, that it ought to be possible to have two separate relationships with them and not be torn between conflicting loyalties. After all, it did not matter to her what actually happened in New Jersey; she had no stake in either version of their move up here. They were here now, and she would know them and take each of them as she found them. It had been silly of her to question Clair; Clair was right. She would have known if something was wrong. They were friends. They shared everything. Beneath the train of her thoughts, her shoulders shifted back and forth against the rough fabric of the driver's seat, trying to escape knowing what Paul had told her.

Clair wondered why Elizabeth seemed so nervous this morning, why she had suddenly not dropped off Colin and Artie. The nonchalance with which Elizabeth deposited the children and ran off to do her work seemed to Clair a measure of the friendship and trust between them, and she wondered first if she had done something to make Elizabeth doubt her. But she couldn't think of anything. Had Paul said something to Elizabeth? For Clair, too, heard Elizabeth drive in every night at one a.m. and she feigned sleep as she felt Paul, night after night, turn, then ease quietly out of the bed, pick up his clothes and go down to the kitchen. She, too, could hear the kitchen door open and shut, quietly, and she had wondered the first night whether he had stood on the porch out of sight to make sure Elizabeth did everything right, or whether he actually went up to check up on her. She thought of speaking to him about it the next morning, but she did not know how to suggest that Elizabeth might be angry, might take offense at his paternal attitude toward her. So she remained silent and waited in bed each night for Paul to return from the barn before she drifted off to sleep again.

At night, Elizabeth confided in Paul. She shared with him her occasional anger at Tom, confessed that she needed the money from the sugaring so that she wouldn't feel so dependent on Tom. After all they weren't his kids, but Edward was giving her almost nothing in child support.

Paul, who once was so critical of Elizabeth's choice to leave her husband, now railed in anger against a man who could deny adequate support to his children. Paul admitted how insecure he had been when he first started to farm, how he was not able to ask many questions because he needed to be confident — for Clair, he said — he needed to be confident and in control. The nightly half hour by the wood stove became an hour, two hours.

"You're a beautiful woman, Elizabeth," Paul said one night, leaning toward her. "Do you have any idea how attractive you are?"

"Oh, sure," Elizabeth said, more lightly than she felt. "In the dark I look great. You can't see the tangles in my hair and my chapped lips and red nose."

Around them the barn odors rose slowly, carried on the draft of the fire, heavily scented with maple. In the firelight, Elizabeth thought, Paul didn't look old or tired, like he did in the day. At night his face seemed gentle and soft.

One night she found herself talking about Anna, compulsively, nervously, telling Paul what she had not yet told herself, that Anna was attracted to her, that she didn't quite know what to make of it, but she was sure that Anna was in love with her.

Paul didn't look surprised. He watched her with his soft, dark eyes as she spoke, not interrupting until she stopped speaking.

"That's too bad," he said.

"What do you mean?" Elizabeth had expected many possible responses as she spoke, but not this one. Then lightly, she added, "Am I so bad to love?" Her voice caught, betraying the casual tone.

"Oh, no." Paul was serious. "I mean I feel sorry for her. It's too bad she's a woman. She's bound to be hurt. You could never feel the same way about her. I mean," he paused and half-laughed as he formed his next thought. "I mean, there's not an abnormal bone in your body. That much, at least, is obvious to me."

She looked at him for a moment, frowning. "I don't think abnormal is a word I'd use. I don't believe. . . "

"Wait a minute," he interrupted. "I don't want to argue about whether it's normal or not." He sidestepped her objection. "I'm talking about you. That's all. I mean," he leaned over very close to Elizabeth's face. "You aren't going to have an affair with her. That's why I feel sorry for her."

His voice, his confidence, caught somewhere inside Elizabeth like the smoke scent trapped in her hair, and she carried both back to bed with her that night.

Now Elizabeth leaned on the goat's pen and waited for Paul to climb the hill to the barn. They had agreed last night that the run was almost over. The buds on the maples seemed to be ripening quickly and they would be making grade C syrup, dark and bitter, if they tapped much longer. And last night they had expressed their pleasure at having, as Paul said, someone special. "I've needed someone special for a long time, someone who understood me, someone I wasn't afraid to talk to."

He was sorry the run was ending, sorry they would only meet in the daytime, lose the rich solitude of their night time talks in the vast darkness of the barn.

Of course he would come tonight. She should have expected it, should have known that he would. In that moment Elizabeth buried inside her the relief she had been feeling that she would not be meeting Paul alone at night, her anticipation that she would be at ease with Clair again once this night time schedule had finished and life had come back to normal.

She saw his shadow loom on the barn roof, then diminish as he stood closer to the fire. Elizabeth did not speak, stood leaning against the pen slats, waiting. His eyes adjusted to the dark. She saw him scan the shadow where she stood. He walked slowly back toward her. He walked to within a few feet of her, stood for a moment, then walked forward again. He leaned over her body, his breath warm in her hair.

"I want you," she heard him say, his voice low and insistent. Then again, "I want you."

She knew she could still turn him around, stop what was happening by slidng aside, flattering him, by using Tom and Clair as buffers. We can never justify this, she could hear herself clearly, for she knew she did not think it justifiable, and yet she did not say the words. Tomorrow, she thought, reaching her hand up to his shoulder, then to the back of his neck, drawing his lips down to hers, tomorrow I'll tell him that. She felt his arms reach around her and secure her firmly in his embrace.

# Chapter 8

Anna's hands gripped the railing around the bucket of the crane and looked down at the receding ground where Chip operated the controls which sent her skyward. For a moment she was eye level with the twigs and branches, a visual fence that laced her in on all sides. Then her head broke, crested, above the tree tops and she felt as though she had become part of the sky.

"How wonderful," she called down to Chip, who stood grinning at her delight. "No wonder you don't mind working out here alone all winter." For she was now at the highest point of the highest hill between two mountain ranges that stretched the length of two different states, and on this day every detail stood out to Anna with a clarity which seemed near hallucinogenic. When she turned to the west she faced the Adirondacks, still snow-capped, awesome in their purple and grey austerity. Behind her were the pine-covered slopes of the Green Mountains, closer, smaller. Between the two ranges, nearly at the bottom of her hill was the long blue of Lake Champlain.

Anna stood quietly for a moment, enjoying the solitude of her splendid height. She wondered – as she tried to trace her path to work through the twisting hills below her – where she would be a year from now, whether any landscape would ever move her as these hills did. She had applied for the few jobs open in her field, knowing how many poets and teachers there were who could fill each one of them. She was beginning to understand that – while she expected to find a job for the next year — it was possible she might not. And if she didn't, how would she be able to go on believing in her own work, believing in herself?

"Can you see the ferry?" Chip's shout interrupted her reverie. "Has it started running yet, or is there still ice on the lake?"

"There's no ice, but I'd need binoculars to make out the ferry," Anna said, peering into the distance.

"Not if you knew what you were looking for," Chip answered.

"Anna, Anna," a child's high voice called.

Anna looked down to see Chip's five year old daughter barrel around the end of the row of trees followed by a young hound dog with floppy ears and long tongue.

"Hi, Shelly. Hi, Tucker," she called down. "Whatcha doin' down there on earth?"

"Let me come up with you. I can go up with her, O.K. Dad?"

Chip glanced up at Anna. "Mind company?"

"No," Anna laughed, "of course not." But she took a last look at the empty sky and the road that wound to nowhere as Chip lowered her back into the orchard.

"Can Tucker come, too?" Shelly asked as Chip handed her up to Anna.

"No," he said firmly. "I want you to hold on to the edge."

She stood leaning against Anna's legs, her nose level with the edge of the bucket. "OOOOh," she breathed, then turned her face up to Anna confidentially. "The branches are neat, but I like it on top best."

"Me, too." She put her hands on Shelly's shoulders and the two stood silently, gazing into the west as the crane bucket rose, then paused, suspending them above the trees once more. Beneath them Chip went back to his work repairing the wire mesh fences around the lower trunk of each tree which kept the hungry mice from gnawing the bark in winter and girdling the tree.

"Come down when you want," he told them. "Just pull your lever toward you."

Anna glanced earthward occasionally. Chip stooped, assiduously knelt and examined each tree, snipping, replacing the fine mesh, pulling back the last weeds of the autumn from around each trunk. His back and shoulders looked broad and competent in the sunlight, but Anna smiled at the damp muddy knees of his bluejeans, knowing he would never notice.

Later they walked together back up the long orchard row to Chip's parked truck.

"Thanks for the lift," Anna said lightly. It had been a lift. She had come home from school, tired, heavily depressed, and went for a long walk, a slow walk to move her away from that depression. Now she felt like a different person, refocused, moved by the commonplace grandeur of the scenery which spread out around her as she rose magically above the tree line.

"Any time," Chip said, enjoying her pleasure. He stooped and picked up a twig. "Here, Tucker," he waved the twig toward the hound, "Fetch."

"Let me, let me, Dad," Shelly insisted, letting go of his hand and running ahead of them with the stick.

"Anyway," Chip turned and looked at Anna for a second, then continued, "anyway, it's been a while since I've seen you out here in the orchard."

"Been a while since you stopped in for a cup of tea," Anna countered instantly, raising an eyebrow and looking back at him. She missed Chip's visits and wondered whether the spring season in the orchard kept him busier than usual, though she thought not, and felt a slight discomfort at bringing it up now.

"Well," he paused awkwardly and Anna knew she was right, it was not just the season. "Seems like you always have company when I go by."

"And you won't come in when there are two women in the kitchen, right?" Anna asked playfully, knowing he was referring to Elizabeth's car parked in her driveway nearly every afternoon in the last two weeks. Chip just shrugged and said nothing. They were nearly at his truck and Shelly was very near.

"You don't like her, do you?" Anna asked in a low voice.

"Not much," he admitted.

"Why?" Anna was curious. She had seen that Chip and Elizabeth did not seem to like one another.

Chip lifted Shelly into the truck cab, then the dog, and shut the door, leaning against it, facing Anna.

"I don't feel like she's honest," he said after a moment. "She never looks at me directly unless she wants me to do something for her."

"Hmmm." Anna realized she was looking at her feet, and looked up suddenly into Chip's open, guileless gaze. She could not doubt him.

"Well, look. I miss seeing you." Her sentences were short, slightly awkward. "So stop in. O.K.?"

"Yup." He looked pleased. "As long as I know I'm welcome."

Anna had seen Elizabeth every day for the two weeks since she kissed her goodnight on the porch of Tom's house. She had waited, the day following that night, to see if Elizabeth would contact her, fearing her need to be with Elizabeth would push the other woman, interfere in her busy life. For the sap had started to run regularly in the first days of March and Elizabeth was at the farm several times a day, emptying the collecting tank, adjusting the fire, finishing the boiling off, pouring, canning. But Elizabeth had pulled into Anna's driveway with Colin and Artie in tow, her hair dishevelled, a humorous look on her face — amused by her own frantic pace. She slogged through the melting snow, one child on each nip, and came ito the small kitchen as though she had a right to be there.

A deep satisfaction had begun to fill Anna then, a sense of warmth and belonging that she had not felt since she was a small child. The isolation which had trapped her for weeks began to lift when she was with Elizabeth. For the first time Anna spoke to another person about her classes — how she could not do the work of preparation, concentrate on a lecture or discussion.

"I'm afraid they'll find me out," Anna confessed.

"What do you mean? Find what out?"

"Find I'm faking, I'm just not there. Today I was in the middle of a discussion about Tennyson and one of my best students was talking and all of a sudden I — like — came-to and realized I hadn't heard a word he had said and I was supposed to respond to him." She paused and ran her hand across her head in a gesture of frustration and weariness, unable to further explain how she felt at these times as though a heavy plate glass had slid down between herself and the rest of the world.

"God. What did you do?"

Anna waved her hand again. "He was a good student. I just said, 'yes, of course, absolutely, Peter,' and then I called on someone else. But that's not it," she insisted, earnest, pleading. "Why is this happening to me? It terrifies me not to be in control of — of my mind."

"Of course it does," said Elizabeth, soothing, practical. "But maybe your mind has just decided it needs a vacation. It hasn't had an easy winter, you know."

"Yeah," Anna had agreed. "But it's my mind and it's going to take a vacation when I give it permission."

Still comforted by the pleasure of seeing Chip, Anna walked down the last row of trees toward her house. Questions of control remained on the surface of her attention. She was able to pay attention in class today, for the first time in weeks, she felt. They had read some sonnets by Christina Rossetti, sonnets about a love which was expected, but never fulfilled. They spoke of what appeared to have been her chosen celibacy.

"Why wouldn't she marry?" the students wanted to know and Anna directed them toward this inquiry.

"Why do you think?" She had turned it around on them: lack of opportunity, lack of desire—was she normal, eccentric, or was it something else?

"She must have been a little weird," one student insisted, and the class exploded with response.

At the end of the hour Anna had to sum it up quickly, show her students all of the connections they were suggesting in just the few moments left to her. She asked them to consider the difficulties of the lives of nineteenth century women, particluarly those who married, bore children. They had noticed that all of the great male authors had been married, but did not realize that not one of the women was when she first started to write, to gain her fame. Anna spoke of Elizabeth Barrett as the only writer who survived, as a writer, being married. Charlotte Bronte, for example, produced nothing in the short term of her married life. It had to be — she could see they were agreeing with her now — a question of control, of a woman's need to control her own time, space, resources. That first.

"Was she weird?" she asked at the end of the class as students gathered their books and jackets.

"No way," came the response of one of her women students. "No way, she just knew where it was at."

Anna laughed and left it at that.

But back in her office, stimulated by the discussion, Anna had looked at the sonnets once again and decided she would begin the next class with another issue of control. She would begin where Rossetti herself began the sonnet sequence.

"Come back to me," she said the words aloud as she walked toward the house in the darkening orchard. "Come back to me, who wait and watch for you; Or come not yet, for it is over then." The poet was saying that the anticipation of meeting the beloved was preferable to the actual meeting. She wanted to ask her class what kind of an environment for love that presupposed. Given the circumstances of her time and class, perhaps Rossetti knew somehow that the love she would prefer for herself was impossibe to fulfill. Perhaps then the dream was better than a reality which only mocked the dream. Anna shook her head, as though to clear her thoughts. She was thinking about Elizabeth, she knew, projecting her own fear of love onto Rossetti. Perhaps she wouldn't talk about it in class tomorrow, feeling so close to home as it did.

"Hey, Rose. Hey, Rose," she called in a musical voice, ducking under the electric wire that made a paddock. "Here's dinner."

She scooped out grain, pulled down a bale of hay and popped the baling twine, fanning out the sheaves. She was hungry herself, nearly lightheaded in the raw March evening, but she was reluctant to go into the house. She could, she knew, drive over to Elizabeth's, eat with her and the children, sit and talk the evening away. It would be good to go over the Christina Rossetti class with Elizabeth, recite those lines again. And yet, she decided, perhaps she would eat alone tonight − "Or come not yet, for it is over then" − she felt stimulated, anticipatory. It was a mood in which she had been used to writing poems, she reminded herself, pausing on the front porch. On either side of her rose the shadows of the two gnarled, aged maples. For years they had been tapped and now, though Chip insisted they were too old for taps, they wept a clear sweet liquid every spring through the unused tap wounds. It was an image she had not been able to use in a poem yet.

She had started a series of poems about the orchard, the trees in the orchard, how they ripened, bore fruit, how in the fall the buds swelled and then held, waiting for spring, protected, sheathed in the most delicate smooth casing. She loved the visualization of the orchard in January, white and black, with an occasional gold or red fruit still hanging from a high bough, left by the pickers because it was too small or unripe, held by the tree for months, a promise stored against the hunger of small rodents who inhabited the orchard. Her images were good, she knew that, but the poems were not — they seemed distant and forced — not as she felt them, but as if they had nothing to do with her life.

She had told Clair she almost never stopped writing poems, but now she was so unsatisfied with her work she was tempted to stop. The source of her poems, her inner life, seemed to Anna to be burbling away on its own, forging new directions, creating images and feelings to which she had access only in her dreams and waking fantasies, not in her conscious working life. When she sat at her desk to write, she could only dredge up cliches and images she had already used in earlier poems. It was frustrating to feel so much and to be able to portray so little. She sighed deeply, picked up two logs from the wood pile stacked on the porch, and went into the house.

She put several records on the stereo and moved absent-mindedly around the small kitchen, preparing a meal for herself. Perched at the kitchen counter, eating warmed over chili and corn muffin, she listened to a woman's voice insist in repeated harmony, "Love has no pride, I call out your name." For the two and half minutes this song lasted, she could sink into her own reverie, create over and over an interior fantasy to go with the lyrics, let the words take her to a place she wanted to go, almost as if the music were the path. At night she would put a record on and masturbate in the dark, finding her way — with repetition—to those interior fantasies, to the source of this erotic energy that plagued and delighted her during the day. At night she would touch her own breasts and imagine them another woman's, imagine another woman's hands touching her, exploring her body as Anna's hands now explored herself. It was not that she had never done this before, but that now the fantasies expanded the physical moment into. . . she was not sure what, but something much more. Energy that had been muted within her for so long was seeping back, charging her like a wire that sparked off of anything she touched.

There was danger and pleasure in this new excitement. She felt the danger most often when she was with others, the pleasure when she was alone as she was now. For with others there was always the chance that she would be mistaken, that she would mistake their response to her, that they would misread her intentions.

She had felt that last night with her student Lee. They had arranged to have dinner together, ostensibly to discuss politics, the women's group, future directions for political action. But Anna admitted a different necessity as soon as the two women sat down at the table. She was surprised at how easily Lee identified herself as a lesbian, spoke of the difficulties she found even among the so-called feminists on a campus so dedcated to imitating Ivy League, heterosexual culture.

Anna sat back to listen, gazing across at the young woman who leaned casually on the table. She was drawn to the softness of her body, the fine bones in her cheeks. Money, she thought, the first time Lee had walked into her office − look how straight those teeth are. But Lee's eyes were never part of her Eastern sophisticate veneer. Anna felt that they were hiding something Lee really wanted to reveal, as they sat across Anna's desk from one another every week for two semesters, consulting about Lee's thesis. Anna didn't feel that concealment now, as she looked across the table at Lee.

When Anna talked about Lee's thesis, her coming graduation, Lee seemed to grow more quiet, almost sad. Anna was surprised. "Aren't you glad of that?" she asked. "I thought this wasn't such a great place for you. Aren't you eager to get out, go someplace you can live you life more openly?"

"Sure," Lee agreed, "but my lover's stuck here for another year. I don't know what that's going to mean."

Anna had seen Lee's lover, a young woman in the theater department, once or twice in productions, sometimes had caught a glimpse of her striking red hair across the campus. Fed on these details, Anna craved more.

"How did you meet her?"

"How? Here at school."

"I mean," Anna paused, not sure what she meant, not sure when she would step over the boundary of what Lee would talk with her about. "How did you know she. . . did you know she was. . . " Anna could see that Lee understood now, was beginning to laugh at her confusion. "So, how did you know you were a lesbian?"

"I fell in love with a woman."

Lee was not going to make it an easy conversation. "Well, I guess that's a start. Were you surprised?"

"Surprised? No. We went from being best friends to being lovers."

"Were you ever with a man?"

"Sometimes, sure," Lee shrugged the admission. "But it was boring."

"Then why the label? I mean, why call yourself a lesbian?"

"It's not a label. It's part of who I am. I've studied history, but I'm an English major. I'm a twenty-one year old college-educated, WASP, lesbian, English major. . . " she paused as though she had given this speech before, could go on with the listing of identities if Anna had not got the point.

She nodded. "O.K. I think I see." Her other questions were locked inside her and would not come out.

Lee looked at her thoughtfully and Anna shifted uncomfortably in her chair, sure a personal question was coming.

"Have you ever loved a woman?" Lee brought the question out, then sat back as though she wanted to distance herself from Anna's answer.

Anna sighed and looked down at the cream swirling in her Irish coffee. Well, why not? It was not as if she had a future at the college to protect. She nodded without looking at Lee.

"When? When you were younger?"

Anna looked up, her face softened. "Now," she confessed. "Now." And with that confidence, she felt her shoulders lighten and her heart trip. It's true, she realized it fully for the first time as she spoke it. It's true. I'm in love with Elizabeth.

But driving home that night the fantasies that threatened to over-whelm her—accelerate her car and pulse in erotic tension—were not of Elizabeth, but Lee. Lee walking throught the orchard with Anna. Lee lying on the hearth while Anna fixed dinner. Lee turning toward Anna, wrestling playfully, Anna pinioned, Lee gently astride her waist as Anna lay on her back, passive. Lee's lips touching Anna's forehead, hair brushing her cheek. Lee's fingers unbuttoning her own blouse, bending over Anna, breasts loose beneath this soft garment. Her hands gentle, unfastening Anna's shirt, seeing the hesitance in Anna's eyes, her voice chiding, "Relax, Professor. It's just about sex, you know." Lee's hands, her lips, breasts, brushing Anna's hands from shoulder to breast to. . . Anna breathing, taking, wanting so deeply. And Anna's silent protest, unregistered. Oh, no, it's not just about sex.

# Chapter 9

Clair lay on her side under the heavy comforter, knees pulled up to her breasts, pain radiating from her center through her body. She adjusted the comforter around her shoulders and shivered as the spasm moved down her spine and into her legs. She thought this would never happen to her again. She hadn't had a period for months, and the agony of this one seemed unfair, unnecessary. A wave of heat flushed through her now, following the pain, but she did not move the comforter, knowing the fever would finish in two or three minutes and she would be cold again. From the noises filtering up to her darkened bedroom, Clair could tell that Sharon and Tammie had finished breakfast and were getting ready to go out to the bus. Chairs scraped on the kitchen floor, the dishwasher door banged shut – Clair flinched at this misuse – and then the kitchen door opened and shut leaving the house in silence.

Cramps had wakened her before dawn and she got up for aspirin, realizing as soon as she was half conscious that Paul was not in the bed, that he had not come to bed again that night, was probably sleeping on the sofa as he had the night before. In her half sleep she had been nauseous and angry, unable at first to separate her pains. She was furious at Paul for doing this, for refusing to come to their bed and refusing to talk about it; and she was furious with her body for this betrayal. Menopause is something doctors make up, she had always maintained; if a woman is healthy and active. . . She groaned under the comforter as another spasm began, her uterus and bowels contracting simultaneously.

Self pity was not part of her repertoire, Clair often told herself, but overwhelmed by this physical disaster, she let herself feel the pity and the pain. No one even knew she was ill, she thought bitterly. Paul had not come into the bedroom for two days and the children never did. When she did not come down to fix their breakfast, they had done it themselves, never thinking to inquire about her. There were many mornings, a few years ago, when Clair had not been able to get out of bed in the morning, and they had learned an early self-sufficiency. They could have at least knocked to see if I were dead or alive, she thought, then realized it wasn't their fault; it was Paul she was furious with and she must not refocus those feelings onto the children. It was Paul.

She knew he had slept with Elizabeth. It was the only explanation for his behavior. And yet she did not want to know it, tried desperately not to know it. I love her, she said wordlessly to herself, huddled under the comforter, I really do love her.

It was not the first time he had slept with one of her friends. She recognized the punishment, distant yet familiar. He hadn't done it to her in years and she rather thought something was changed between them—in recent years especially — thought he might have found some other way of working out his feelings of anger at her. For he was angry with her, she knew that, angry that she was not everything he wanted her to be, angry that she had the breakdown and been hospitalized, forcing him into a kind of care and concern he did not want to have to give. He loved her, she believed that too, but he loved her whole and competent and complementary to himself, filling his needs and empty spaces. He did not love her when she was inadequate, when she was absent from him.

"It's not your father's fault, Clair, you can't be angry with him" she heard her mother's voice. "He just wasn't meant to be cooped up with a family. Your father always had his own way, just what he wanted. He came to expect it. You can't blame him, his mother brought him up that way. I don't need to blame him. So you had better get over feeling that way."

And she had learned not to blame her friends. She knew what women needed in a man. She knew Pauls's warmth and intelligence and sensitivity, how attractive his little-boy eyes and droopy, vulnerable mouth were to women, to many women who weren't used to being seen by men at all. Paul never looked through or around a woman he wanted; he knew how to look directly into her eyes and speak to her. She could not blame Elizabeth. But—a different pain shook her body now, radiating from a different center — she did love Elizabeth, really love her, she said over and over. She felt this betrayal differently and she did not know how she would bear this loss, could not think how she would bear it. Caught in a drowziness of pain and aspirin haze, she dozed fitfully under the winter comforter.

In her dreams she was a lonely child playing on the long back hall staircase, a green tunnel that led down and down past barred doors and sacks of refuse, the detritus of lives, carefully gathered together and stacked for Monday morning pickup. She went down and down, winding around each banister post at the turn in the stairs until she came to the door, the large iron door that led to the basement, a vast darkness looming before her when she peered into it.

She walked for a long time in the dark, walked forward, not crawling or feeling anxiously for the walls, but walked upright and straight forward, though she could not see the ground or her feet, nor — for a long time—could she see a light ahead of her. Gradually she walked into the light, a soft haze of silver-gold which reflected the sand under her feet. For she was on a beach, Clair realized in the dream and drew satisfaction from this recognition. Ahead of her were dunes and rocks, rounded like bread rising. Then she turned a corner and walked into direct light shining on the most spectacular waves breaking, casting huge spires of azure spray into the air. Awestruck, she stood for a moment, absorbing the color with her eyes, inhaling it with every breath, letting it seep into her body as the color touched her skin.

But this was not a place to stay. She looked and looked and then turned and walked back out of the sunlight, back through the mist and into the darkness, walked with joy and peace, feeling, yes, this is what the end of a journey should be, not a final destination, but a place to pause, a gift of vision before we begin again.

She woke slowly, bringing the dream to consciousness with her, holding carefully to these final emotions as she woke to awareness of where she was, felt around her body for the pain. The cramps had subsided, leaving only the pain of loss. And she knew she would live with that pain for much longer.

Clair turned over under the covers, thinking she would get up and shower and face the day, when she heard Paul come into the kitchen from the barn. She heard the chair at the table scrape once, then again, as he sat, stood up. His heavy step sounded on the stairs. He was coming up to see her. Panicked for a moment, she huddled under the comforter. What did he want? Why was he coming now, she asked without wondering why now might be different than later?

The door opened. He paused and she peered out at him. She saw bright light behind him in the hall. He cleared his throat. She did not speak.

"Are you all right?" His voice, trying for concern, betrayed nervousness.

"Cramps," she refused more information.

"Cramps! I thought you were over that."

"Over it?" Clair echoed. "No, I'm not over it."

"Do you need anything?" He could fall into their old pattern now that he knew her complaint was physical. She had better not need anything.

"No. I'll be getting up in a while." She wanted him to leave, and he turned and pulled the door shut behind him, letting it click softly.

She heard him walk down the stairs, but before he reached the bottom, she heard the kitchen door open and a voice – it was Elizabeth's, she knew the tone at once – called a greeting. Elizabeth's voice. What was she doing here, Clair wondered, how could she come here now?

"What are you doing here?" Paul asked, coming down the stairs and walking quickly into the kitchen to face Elizabeth.

She seemed surprised. "I came to see Clair and have my morning cup of coffee. Why? Is something wrong?"

Elizabeth was suddenly anxious. Why was Paul looking at her like that? She told him yesterday when he phoned that they couldn't go on meeting, that Clair was her friend, that Tom was important to her – and jealous. She didn't see how they could go on.

Paul's eyes filled with intensity and meaning as he looked at Elizabeth. He reached for her hand, but she pulled away and asked again, "Where is Clair? Is something wrong, Paul?"

"Cramps," he said briefly. "She doesn't feel well. She hasn't gotten up yet this morning."

"Oh, lord," Elizabeth said with instant compassion. "Have you taken her up something hot?" At Paul's negative gesture, she grabbed the kettle from the stove and went to the sink to fill it. "It's been months since she had a period. She must feel awful."

She put the kettle on the burner and turned to face Paul, leaning against the stove. She could tell he saw the assertion and distance in her stance.

Paul sat at the kitchen table. "She knows," he said dramatically, an attempt to bring Elizabeth toward him.

"You told her?" Elizabeth's voice was low and shocked.

Paul shook his head, morose. "She knows."

"What do you mean?" Elizabeth was exasperated with him and fearful. Paul was staring at her with his large mournful eyes. "Look, Paul," she could not wait for him to volunteer the information, she needed to know. Her voice was demanding. "What do you mean, she knows? Why do you think she knows? What does she know?" She walked over to the table where he sat and stood next to him, over him.

"I couldn't help it," he said, reaching again for Elizabeth's hand. She pulled away. "I was so caught up in what was happening to us." He paused trying to see sympathy in her eyes. "I couldn't think about anything but you. I haven't thought of anything else for days." Still Elizabeth said nothing, but stood looking down at him, waiting.

"I couldn't sleep with her, after," his voice caught, husky, "after us."

"What do you mean, you couldn't sleep with her? You mean she wanted you to make love with her and you couldn't?"

He shook his head again and looked sheepish. How did he get such droopy eyelids, Elizabeth wondered as she gazed at him, and then, how did I ever get involved in this?

"No," he confessed. "I couldn't go up and get in her bed after being with you. So I've been sleeping on the sofa."

"Oh, jesus," Elizabeth sank heavily into a chair across the table from Paul. She should have known. But how could she? She had told him on the phone that nothing was changed, that she was Clair's friend and Tom's woman. It never occurred to her that he wouldn't obey her, like one of the children. She assumed Paul could be managed, and she began to realize as she sat looking at him that he would not be managed.

"I'm in love with you," Paul said, leaning across to her, his face earnest. "That may not be O.K. with you, but I'm in love with you and," he drew a shadow across the earnestness, "the thought of you sleeping with that, that disgusting idiot," he paused as though words had deserted him at the memory of Tom, "of you having to go up and get in his bed, darling," he rushed on, "I want you." His words were urgent. "I want to live with you and be with you always." He stopped abruptly.

Elizabeth was staring at him, her eyes wide. "What's wrong?" he asked, half laughing, teasing, "You're not surprised, are you? I told you in the barn, that night you asked that it wasn't hard to love you."

Elizabeth sat, for the first time speechless, sifting her feelings as she tried to hear what Paul was saying. She was flattered, as she had been flattered by his attention from the first. When she compared him to Tom and Edward, both so insensitive in their different ways, both so casual about her presence in their lives, Paul seemed very special.

The tea kettle on the stove started to steam, then whistle. Elizabeth jumped up, turned off the burner and put some tea in the pot, pouring the steaming water over it. Then she settled Clair's tea cozy over the pot and turned back to Paul. He might be special, but she didn't want a man she could not control.

"So what are you saying, Paul? You want to divorce Clair and marry me? Now? Right now?" She leaned against the stove and crossed her arms over her chest again. "Live with me and my five children?"

"I haven't worked out all the details. I'm too involved in being in love with you." He smiled warmly up at her, as though her question belied her stance.

"But let's be practical. We can't just destroy two other relationships if we don't mean something by it."

"It means we're in love," he included her this time, she noticed. "It would be dishonest not to admit how we feel."

There was temptation here, Ellizabeth felt that, as she stood thinking, waiting. It would be exciting to throw up her hands and say to the world, yes, I'm overwhelmed, I love him. It would be chaotic, the village would churn with gossip. Tom would be frantic in his injured pride and rage – she could imagine his response, knew it would be violent in some dramatic way, though not, she assumed violent toward her. And Clair would be. . . Clair would be what? Her mind began to close the excitement down. She knew what Clair would be, knew what she was now, solitary, lying alone upstairs listening to the sound of her voice and Paul's, not knowing what they were saying–Clair would never know what the village was saying either – but she would wait, she would wait and take what came to her. And the children. If Paul meant nothing by this, where would she go with five children?

She leaned toward Paul. "I'm not in love with you, Paul." Her voice was firm and urgent. "And I don't think you're in love with me. We got caught up in something. It was nice, it was special. But I can't let it destroy my life." She knew without hearing it what Paul would say.

He said it anyway. "Darling, we can't think about others. We have to do what we need to do." He stood finally, propelled by the sense that she was escaping him and moved toward her. She turned away from him and took two cups down from the cupboard over the stove. Paul embraced her from behind, his hands and lips urgent, trembling over her vulnerable places. She felt the warmth of passion begin, and the warmth of anger.

"Paul stop it." She was angry. She elbowed him aside and picked up the teapot and mugs. "I'm going to take some tea up to Clair." She turned and walked toward the stairs, as he stood by the stove, wordless.

Elizabeth was afraid for a moment that he would follow her, then her anxiety began to focus instead on the top of the stairs. She was climbing the stairs on an impulse, a gesture of care and a gesture – to Paul – of her autonomy. She was climbing the stairs because she had begun something when she filled the tea kettle, boiled the water, settled the cozy. She was caught in habit, in the everydayness of the details of fixing the tea, in the assumption of nurturing a friend who was in pain. She was climbing the stairs, she realized as she came to the landing and turned up to the second half of the flight, because if she did not climb them now, she would never be able to climb them later. Whatever Clair knew or thought had to be tenuous, partially realized. Elizabeth knew her behavior could confirm or deny or allay Clair's fears.

At the top, she paused. She wanted to flee, to turn and run down the stairs and out to her car and drive away from this tension. She drew a deep breath, walked down the long hall, and knocked lightly on Clair's door.

Clair lay in the dark and listened as Elizabeth began to climb the stairs. She pulled her head under the comforter, not wanting to hear the slow deliberate tread. Why? Why was she coming up here now, Clair wondered, then, biting her lip, she felt the shame of inadequacy, the humiliation of her position. They had been equal, she and Elizabeth had shared their lives and thoughts as equals and now – now Clair had been somehow dispossessed. She felt she had lost her place, her right to be in the world. She huddled under the comforter, hoping Elizabeth would turn around, would go back down the stairs when she saw the door was shut, the room dark. But she heard Elizabeth's steps come down the hall and heard her knock on the door and — because she had almost never denied anyone anything they had asked from her — Clair could not say what she felt.

Instead of shouting, go away, she said in a low, nearly inaudible voice, "Come in."

Elizabeth pushed open the door, saw the darkness in the room, and Clair's body huddled under the comforter. "I've brought you some tea," she said, the strain not showing in her voice. "Paul said you hadn't had anything hot yet this morning and," she set the tea pot and mugs on the bedside stand, "I thought you'd probably need it."

Clair peered out from under the comforter. "You brought me tea?" She was touched, and slightly confused by this gesture.

"Mmmm, hmmm." Elizabeth sat on the edge of the bed. "Want me to pour?"

"Yes," Clair pulled herself upright and puffed a pillow behind her back. "Yes, there's nothing I need so much right now as a cup of tea." She spoke the words as if she were just discovering them.

"Was it bad?" Elizabeth asked, tossing her hair out of her eyes as she poured the tea.

Clair looked at her for a moment, still not able to readjust to this tone, this Elizabeth who was so much the same, but so different from what she had expected when she heard the knock on the door. She must mean the cramps, surely she wouldn't be asking about Paul's defection from her bed.

She nodded, "Yeah, and what a surprise." Her shoulders hunched up, remembering the pain.

Elizabeth handed her the tea and looked soberly into Clair's eyes from under the shock of hair that fell forward. Does she mean me? How much could Clair know or suspect? But she decided to take the surface meaning from Clair's words and in that moment the two women established a kind of truce, a temporary reconfirmation of loyalties.

"I'm not looking forward to it myself," Elizabeth said.

They sat, two women perched on the bed, hands cupped around hot mugs of tea, for another ten minutes, then Elizabeth stood to leave. She leaned over and gave Clair a brief hug. "Call me if you need anything," and she was gone.

Clair sat, propped up on a pillow, sipping her tea, staring at the sharp ray of morning light coming in between the curtains. Nothing in her previous experience had prepared her for this morning. She could not know all of Elizabeth's fears as she climbed the stairs — afraid to go forward, but more afraid to go back — but she sensed some the the the nervousness under Elizabeth's customary, straightforward warmth. She guessed she could assume this was not easy for Elizabeth either. But what did it mean, she wondered, anxious and yet reluctant to dispel the haze of humiliation and self-blame with which she had surrounded herself in the last two days. For Clair was accustomed to blaming herself when life failed her.

All she knew today was that the humiliation was not really there. She did not know why, but it was not. She felt sad, she still felt the loss with which she had awakened, but she did not, for the moment, feel ashamed.

She set the mug on the table next to the bed and threw off the comforter. Her legs were weak, but serviceable. She stood and stretched. Her body ached from shoulders to knees with the aftermath of pain. Clair walked toward the bathroom. When she opened the door, she was flooded with bright light. It filled every crack and crevice, glanced off of the tiles and porcelain and chrome, shocking her for a moment with its intensity. As she turned on the taps, letting her eyes adjust to this light, she remembered her dream, the shock of the light as she had stepped into the sun, the brilliance of the azure spray. Bemused, she replayed that scene for herself as she took off her robe, tested the heat of the water. Her painter self was adjusting the light and contrast of the scene, focusing the textures and colors before she even realized she would like to try and paint — not the scene itself — but some sense of the combination of light and shadow which had given her such a sense of peace and joy as she woke from her dream. She had that canvas stretched downstairs in the closet. But when she thought of that, she was immediately aware of Paul again, and the pleasure in the contemplation of work turned to tension and anxiety. She would never, she knew as she stepped into the hot shower, never again paint in this house.

# Chapter 10

Anna walked into her office as the phone was shrilling. She considered not answering. It was four o'clock on a Friday afternoon and she was tired, ready to leave for home, but duty, habit and curiosity moved her toward the ringing.

"Hello?"

"Anna?" She was surprised to hear Elizabeth's voice. She had never called at the office before. "Can you come over tonight? For dinner, I mean?"

"Yeah, I'd love to. What's wrong?"

"Ohh," she sighed. "It's just been a rough couple of days. I'd love to see you. I'll tell you all about it then, O.K.?"

"Sure," Anna agreed. "I've got some news, too. Something to celebrate."

"Great. Stop for a bottle of wine, then, on your way out."

Anxiety, elation and fear pushed at Anna as she sorted through the unopened mail on her desk, stacked ungraded papers in a single pile to put in her brief case, and rearranged her class notes for the file folder.

The call had come just before noon, the department secretary running down the hall to tell her it was long distance and they couldn't transfer it. It was from Oregon. And they offered her a job. Her application had been one of several they selected. They couldn't ask her out for an interview, the man said, since it was a one year job. She could have a week to decide.

Anna was thrilled. The salary was decent; they had liked her manuscript of poems; Oregon had a good writing program. But almost at once, the edge of her anticipation was marred by the realization that she would have to leave Elizabeth. Could she just do that? Or could she finally talk with Elizabeth about what Anna was sure they felt between them? She had imagined for weeks what she might say to Elizabeth if a job offer came through – "Oh, by the way, I won't go if you want me to stay," or, "Why don't you come with me?" – although she couldn't imagine how Elizabeth could do that. The divorce was not settled; there was Tom. And, a voice chided her, you don't even know that Elizabeth feels what you feel. How about first things first?

Anna was staring aimlessly at the neatened piles on her desk when a hesitant tap sounded on her office door. It was Lee.

"Hey, I heard about the job offer. Congratulations. You must be pleased, huh? Will you take it?"

"I don't know," Anna admitted. "But I am really pleased. And relieved."

"Well, why wouldn't you take it then?"

Why indeed? Anna leaned back in her chair and rested her feet on her desktop. "Well, there is Elizabeth." She was testing, hoping to see in Lee's response some reflection of her own reality.

Lee dropped into a chair and looked serious. "Really? Couldn't she just come with you?"

Anna was startled at the directness with which her own thought came back to her. It might be possible, then. She ventured further. "Well, she has five children." There. What would Lee – in her willful, sophisticated clarity – make of that?

"Five children?" Lee seemed flabergasted, over-reacting a bit to heighten the drama of her surprise. "*Five* children?"

Anna was smiling at Lee's confusion, but her smile faded when Lee went directly to the concommitant point. "And she's got a husband?" Her voice was disapproving now.

"No," but Anna had to admit, "a resident boyfriend."

"Oh." Lee settled back in her chair and looked at Anna, her head cocked to one side. "I thought you were involved in something that was possible. I mean, I really thought you meant to get it on with this woman."

Anna felt her face start to flush. She hated the jargon these kids used she said to herself, but that was not the only reason for her chagrin. She was defensive now. "Well, he's usually not there during the week." That was a little lie, she realized as she said it, Tom had been coming home more and more frequently in the last few weeks. How had she gotten herself into this conversation, anyway, she wondered?

"But what's her commitment?" Lee asked, pushing. Then she retreated. "She sounds like a straight woman. That's all I mean. It can be hard, getting involved with a woman who's really thinking about men all the time."

"I guess I really don't know about commitment," Anna admitted. "But it's not always that simple." She would speak to Elizabeth tonight, she resolved. She had to know what Elizabeth felt.

The two women walked out of the office together, through the long airless hall and out into the spring sunset. Anna felt her body lighter than it had been in months and she breathed in the cold damp air with pleasure. They paused by Anna's car, Lee turning to walk downtown.

"Well, have a nice evening," Lee said doubtfully as she walked away.

Elizabeth and the children and Anna all toasted her job offer. Anna's nervous anticipation of talking with Elizabeth turned the wine slightly bitter on her tongue as she sipped. Elizabeth was too unambivalently pleased, she thought, and then chided herself. Elizabeth had suffered with her through the firing, through the difficult spring job search. Why should she not be pleased? It was Shanna who voiced what Anna was thinking.

"Is Oregon near to here?"

"No, dummy," said Larry, scathingly superior, "it's on the west coast of the United States and Vermont is on the east coast."

Shanna looked puzzled. "Is Anna going away, then?"

Anna caught Elizabeth's eye for a moment, not quite able to interpret the look she saw there. Rueful? Laughing? Was there any regret?

"Maybe," Anna said, leaning across the table toward Shanna's puzzled, frowning face. "I may have to move to Oregon, so I can teach school there."

"Why can't you teach school here?" Shanna demanded, unappeased, willing to be difficult.

Anna shrugged. How could she explain it, she wondered, when it didn't make sense to her either?

After dinner and dishes and a seemingly endless round of goodnights, Anna and Elizabeth settled in front of the fire.

"The children will miss you," Elizabeth said quietly.

"Won't you?" Anna asked before she knew she would speak.

"Of course," said Elizabeth. "That goes without saying."

Anna awkwardly shifted her weight in the big overstuffed chair. Tonight she could not seem to find the hollows her bones were accustomed to settling into. Elizabeth looked nervous to Anna, troubled, less at ease than she could ever remember her being.

"What's wrong?" she asked after a pause. "You said on the phone it had been a rough two days. What's up?"

Elizabeth had been waiting for, and dreading, this moment since she had called Anna earlier in the day. For she didn't want to tell Anna what had been happening in the last few days and yet she needed to tell her. She needed to tell someone who could help her sort throught the details, examine her expectations, her assumptions, assess the damage and foretell the future.

She began abruptly. "Paul's in love with me." She looked in the fire, not at Anna.

"What?" Anna's voice registered her incredulity, as Elizabeth had expected. When Elizabeth did not answer, Anna assumed she must be joking. "Well," she said lightly. "Poor Paul."

"What?" Elizabeth asked sharply, realizing as she said it that her words and tone were parroting Anna's; realizing, too, that her first response was to ask, as she had just a few days ago, am I so bad to love? She was still staring at Anna.

"I just meant I didn't think you even liked Paul, nor he you, so it seemed an unhappy disposition of his affections, if he is indeed 'in love with you.'" Anna's voice became distant and formal and her tone put the last words she spoke in deliberate quotation marks. She was waiting for Elizabeth to say, yes, you're right, I can't stand him, waiting for her to somehow explain how Paul's feelings toward her could have changed from hostility to love since they had last spoken of him.

"Don't make this hard for me, Anna," Elizabeth begged, sitting forward, resting her arms on her knees. "It's a mess. I don't know what's what."

Anna felt the back of her neck go chill, held herself quiet while the sensation worked its way down her spine to her gut. It was fear, she realized, as though she were at a great distance from her body, observing.

"So tell me what happened," she said, neutralizing her voice, hearing Lee's words playing over and over in the base of her skull — but what's her commitment, that's all, what's her commitment?

"Start at the beginning," she said. "I think I have to hear the whole thing."

Elizabeth tried. And Anna tried to hear, but she found herself becoming more and more angry as she listened. "Why didn't you tell him to fuck off that first night when he came out to check on you?" she asked Elizabeth, unwilling to imagine the reality that seemed so simple in Elizabeth's answer.

"It was his barn. How could I tell him to go away?"

It was his male prerogative, too, Anna felt, that allowed him to court, to impose hinself and his affections, even when they were so clearly not returned. Not returned at first, that is, for now Elizabeth was confessing that she had come to enjoy his presence, his conversation.

Committed, Elizabeth told the story to Anna, carried forward by having begun, but with a growing awareness of Anna's jealousy, her hostility. The control made her weary, always keeping certain things back, hiding some of her impetuous and willing reponses to Paul. Why did it all have to be so complicated, she wondered, as she carefully picked her way through the events of the last two nights in the barn. How much can I admit? Her face and body softened, her gestures became vulnerable as she appealed to Anna's sympathy and her love, not willing to lose either.

"I did care for him." Her voice was low, barely a whisper. "I need something for my life. I guess I don't really know what it is, but for a minute it seemed like it might be him."

"But what about Clair?" Anna could not help but ask.

"Well, of course, that's it, isn't it?" Elizabeth sat up, brisk and matter of fact again, confident in her sacrifice. "I mean, it's just impossible and I told him so."

Anna felt the muscles in her face and jaw begin to relax. She had not been sure what the end of this tale would be when Elizabeth was telling the middle of it, and now she felt comforted, partially reassured by Elizabeth's assurance. She wanted to reach out and touch Elizabeth, but the two women sat in separate chairs, pulled up to the coffee table in front of the fireplace. For Anna to move toward Elizabeth would have required a deliberate and obvious effort, an effort she was not able to make. To one side of the coffee table stretched the large and comfortable sofa, and she wondered why they never sat there. They always moved toward these separate chairs when they walked into the living room.

Anna felt the fire was too warm tonight. The usually drafty living room seemed close and stuffy, as though all that Anna was feeling was trapped tightly within its four walls.

"Does Clair know?" she asked Elizabeth. "About how Paul feels?" She assumed not.

But Elizabeth hesitated before she answered. "I don't know. I mean Paul hasn't told her, but," she paused and Anna waited, wondering. "But Paul's being a fool. I told him it wouldn't do, but he still thinks it will." Her voice was exasperated. "He called this afternoon and said he was coming over here tonight."

"Really?" Anna was surprised, angry again.

"Isn't that crazy?" Elizabeth mollified her. "I told him you would be here and Tom would be home by midnight."

"What did he say?"

"I *love* you." Elizabeth made her voice low and dramatic, mocking. Really, she thought, it was ludicrous. He was so self-dramatizing.

"He's really dramatizing this," she said outloud to Anna.

"Yeah, it seems self-centered. He must have been needing some attention. Do you think Clair notices anything weird in his behavior?"

"That's what I worry about," Elizabeth admitted. "I went over there this morning and she was in bed with cramps and he hadn't even taken her any tea." She was indignant, then added, "and while I was making the tea, he wanted to make out in the kitchen," she shook her head, "like he couldn't contain himself or something."

"How can you keep going over there?" Anna asked angrily. "It sounds awful." She pulled her knees up and wrapped her arms around them, trying to contain her feelings. What was going on here? It didn't make any sense at all. How could Elizabeth be smiling about this?

"Why do you go there?" she asked again.

"I have to, for Clair's sake." She realized that might not make any sense at all to Anna. "Did you know about Clair's breakdown?" Anna shook her head, not speaking. "Paul told me about it. I sort of knew from some things Clair had let drop once or twice, but I didn't realize how bad it had been."

94

"Elizabeth, don't you think that's a real violation of confidence? How could he tell you that?"

"I don't know. I don't think it was. I am her friend and if there's something I should know to help her. . . "

"Right, you're her friend," Anna interrupted. "And if she needed help, don't you think she would have asked you? Or told you?"

She thought she was beginning to see what had happened between Elizabeth and Paul, how he had brought her into an alliance, a confidence. They had held a secret between them a secret that somehow bound Elizabeth to him.

Elizabeth could hear the annoyance in Anna's voice again and felt her own irritation and weariness creep back. "Get off it, Anna," she said sharply. "If Paul's my friend, he needs to be able to tell me things, just like Clair does. I can't help it if they happen to be married to one another."

Anna was about to retort when the phone rang. Elizabeth rose and went into the kitchen. Anna sat thinking. What was it in Elizabeth's words that had upset her? Paul's my friend, she had said. It was in the present tense. It wasn't over. Whatever Elizabeth was saying, Anna didn't think it was really over. She could hear Elizabeth's voice rising in the next room, angry, then soft again.

"Guess who?" she asked when she came back into the living room and dropped heavily into her chair.

"Paul?"

"Yeah. He wanted to come over. I told him you were here."

I'm her life insurance, Anna thought to herself, that's why she called me this afternoon. "What did he say to that?"

Elizabeth started to laugh, then groaned ruefully. "It's not funny. He said he thought he'd just come over and sit on the front steps for awhile so he could be closer to me?" Her voice rose on an inflection and then she started to laugh again. Anna felt some bubble of hilarity rise in her, too, in spite of wanting to keep her anger close, and it rose and broke and the two women sat laughing, the tension between them moving out to the surface of their laughter.

"God, what a fool he is," Elizabeth finally gasped.

"Maybe Tom will trip over him when he comes home," Anna suggested and they both went off in another wave of laughter.

"Look," Anna said, finally sober for a moment. The room seemed to be comfortable again, the space between floor and ceiling quite adequate to contain what she was feeling. "I understand that he's in love with you." Indeed, she thought she understood it only too well. "But you have to tell me. How did you come to be close to him? I mean, confess. A month ago you didn't like him. You told me he was opinionated. What else? Egotistical?"

Elizabeth nodded, accepting the charge, feeling the change in Anna's tone of voice. She sat reflecting for a moment. What had it been, she wondered? She had always felt defensive around Paul, like she was a small child who couldn't do or say anything important or correct.

"I think it must have been that he changed his mind about me," she said finally. "He seemed to want to talk to me. He started listening to what I had to say."

She did not feel as open in telling this to Anna as she might have a few weeks ago, felt again the check of Anna's caring, felt surrounded and weighted for a moment by all of this wanting — at once so flattering and so suffocating.

"I've never known a man before who listened like that, a man I felt I could say anything to."

"Was it so different from the kinds of things we talk about?"

"Different? Yes. It's always different when you're talking to a man." She added hastily, "Not better, I mean, but — I don't know — more intense, somehow."

Anna sat frowning in her chair, trying to sort through the meaning of Elizabeth's words. The meaning was not clear to her, not clear at all, and she was not sure whether the confusion was accidental or deliberate.

Elizabeth saw the frown and felt the distance. She groped for the words that would bring Anna back to her. "I told him about us," she said impulsively.

"You what?" Anna's words were sharp. She sat staring at Elizabeth, unable to imagine what she meant.

Elizabeth realized something was even more wrong than it had been before she had spoken. "About how close we are," she elaborated, "about what a good friend you've been to me." And then she said — later she could not remember whether she had been pushed to it by longing or anguish, by caring or dread—she said, "I told him I thought you were the most attractive woman I'd ever known and if I ever had an affair with a woman, it would be you." The words finished in a rush and there was a silence in the room neither woman could break easily.

Anna heard the fire crackle and hiss and felt the blood rushing to her head, felt the adrenalin spill out and speed up her heart and breath, though she sat silent, not daring to move or speak.

Elizabeth's mind was rushing ahead, urged by her impulsive twisting of words to reconstruct a story to tell to Anna. She hadn't exactly told Paul that, though she knew it was true when she spoke it, knew, although she would never admit this to Anna, that it was what their closeness had been about for these last months. Anna's in love with me, she had said to Paul, and now she had said the other half, I'm attracted to Anna. But it couldn't mean anything real, she insisted to herself as she sat watching Anna and the fire, it was just part of their closeness, to wonder at, perhaps to comment on, as they were now. That was all.

When Anna spoke, her words were calm, deliberate, "Don't you think you might have mentioned this to me before you told Paul about it?" She looked directly at Elizabeth. Anna felt her heart slow as she spoke, begin to beat very slowly and strongly.

"Why?"

Anna stared. How could Elizabeth not understand? How could she put what she was feeling into words? That this was the end of something, this speaking aloud, and she did not know why or what or how it had happened like this.

"Why?" She shrugged. "It just seems that it's something private between us and I can't believe you told him about it, but wouldn't tell me."

"But, Anna, I've just told you." Elizabeth seemed exasperated, as though Anna were one of the children, deliberately misunderstanding to get more attention from her.

Anna thought for another moment. "So what did he say when you told him?"

Elizabeth looked up sharply. She couldn't tell Anna that. "Not much. What could he say? He didn't say, how awful, if that's what you mean."

"So was this before or after he came on to you?" Anna couldn't keep the anger down any longer. And she realized as soon as she asked the question that the answer was irrelevant, that whether before or after, Elizabeth had been using their feelings for one another to create an atmosphere—an atmosphere of trust, perhaps, but also an atmosphere of sexual tension. How could Paul have failed to rise to that bait, she wondered bitterly?

"What difference does it make?" Elizabeth's voice was rising too. "I thought — I just told you because I wanted you know that I care about you, that I'm not ashamed of my feelings. What's wrong with that? What's wrong with you?"

"What's wrong with me?" Anna stood, her voice shaking with anger and tears. "What's wrong with me is that I love you, damn it." She was facing Elizabeth, shouting the words. "I love you, I want you. I want to be with you, to hold you. . . " she could not go on.

"But, Anna, I love you too. I've just said so." Elizabeth sat with her knees pulled up, arms wrapped around them. She looked up at Anna's grief, but did not reach out to her.

"But you *slept* with Paul." She hadn't known that, but saw as soon as the accusation was out that she was right. "You slept with him and you won't make love with me. That's the message, isn't it?"

"Yes." Elizabeth rose to face Anna, her voice pitched to match. "Yes, that's the message. I just can't do that." She could not believe this was happening to her, to their friendship. What was wrong with everyone, she wondered. All anyone seemed to think about was sex. She never wanted to have to deal with sex again, she thought with anger, and in the same moment wished Tom home, wished all of the complications to end in his unambiguous presence.

"It isn't about sex, Anna." She could insist on that. "We're friends. Just because we have physical feelings about one another doesn't mean we have to act on them." Her voice was pleading for peace between them.

"I just can't do that," she repeated. She stared across at Anna and felt afraid. Her skin felt thin and fragile, as though it could be shattered now by a word, cracking her control, leaving her to spill out around the edges.

They stood for a long moment like that, eyes locked, and then Anna sank wearily into her chair again. "Well," she said, her head dropped into her hand, her eyes covered, "if you can't, I guess it's just as well that I know where we stand." She looked up again. "I wanted more for us than that. You knew that."

Elizabeth was cautious. "I do now," was all she would admit.

Anna rose again, slowly this time. "Look, I think I'll go now. I want to be alone. And I don't want to be here when Tom gets home."

Elizabeth nodded, relieved. "Call me tomorrow?"

"Whenever."

She walked slowly to the car, her feet weighted by the heavy March mud, her shoulders bent forward. She did not cry, her feelings had sunk too deeply for tears to come easily. She walked unaware of her surroundings, walked to the car and opened the door and drove out the drive to the long road which wound up the hill to the orchard, knowing that she had spoken her love for a woman in anger, not in tenderness, feeling that to the core of herself. But she did not know why it had happened like that. She drove away from Elizabeth toward her own house, her solitude and protection. She drew a deep breath, as though she had been swimming under water a long way, and thought to herself with grim irony, well, at least I didn't trip over Paul on the way out the front door. It was not a comfort.

# Chapter 11
## April

Clair snapped the sheet sharply in the brisk April wind and fumbled in her pocket for a clothespin. The sun was warm this morning and the air smelled damp and green. As she moved down the clothesline, stretching, pinning the brightly colored winter shirts, the heavy sets of long underwear, she felt for the first time that spring was possible, hoped that the next time she hung these clothes out, it would be to fold them and put them into the cedar chest until next winter. I should be doing something about the garden, she thought, as the warmth of the spring sun settled on her shoulders. The seeds had arrived during sugaring and she had tucked them in a cupboard, thinking to herself she would take them out in a couple of weeks and plant some starts in her south window. And she had filled a few flats with potting soil, poking some tomato and broccoli seeds randomly into the soil, unable to be very precise or caring about this planting. The seeds sprouted as haphazardly as they were planted, two or three in the first week, then a dozen tall, nodding dots of green on long white stems. But she did not remember to water them, leaving them for three days, then rescuing them with a drenching and vowing to be more careful. It was a week before she thought of them again and by then the soil had dried to powder and the thin stems drooped like fine hairs over the edge of the flats.

She had thought in March she would not have a garden this year, that she never wanted to have to nurture anything again. The responsibility seemed more than she could accept, those vulnerable, desiccated little plants were a reproach to her for her entire life. How could she have begun them and then abandoned them? It was unfair and unlike herself, usually so careful of her duties, fulfilling them in form, if not in spirit.

As she stood at the end of the line, empty clothes basket at her feet, Clair wondered if she shouldn't go in and start another set of seeds. It wasn't too late, at least six weeks before things could be set out for the summer. She walked over to the garden, a medium-sized, plowed piece of land where she had toiled in the summers. She supposed the work had given her some pleasure, though it was difficult for her to separate her sense of necessity — that this was what she ought to do, was expected to do—from her pleasure in doing the right thing. And she couldn't quite separate that from any pleasure she might have taken in the work itself. Clair sighed heavily, chilled for a moment by this realization. She supposed the only way one could separate duty from desire would be to do only things that were forbidden. She thought about that for a moment. If someone told her not to garden, would she have been able to distinguish the pleasures in it, the warmth of the soil, the smell of tomato leaves on her hands after an hour of pruning? But it was an idle speculation. She always did what was expected of her. Not to do so created unmanageable anxiety. She leaned on the garden gate and stared at nothing. She really ought to go in and start some more plants.

As she turned away, warm sun drew her up the hill toward the stand of maple trees. She was alone on the farm this morning. Paul had taken the children to town for Saturday shopping and there was no one here to need her. She climbed slowly, feeling the pull of unaccustomed muscles in her calves, a slow ache start in her lungs as she breathed more deeply in the spring air.

At the edge of the woods, she stood and looked down at the farm. There were no half lights in April, she realized, no leaf shade, no shadow of vegetation, just the stark white sun and the absolute dark where the sun could not reach. At this midmorning hour, the sun cast a thin dark line up the side of the house and barn, flattened the rest of the landscape in glare. Chiaroscuro. The word from one of her first painting classes flashed through her thoughts as she stared down at the landscape. Chiaroscuro. Clair-obscure. She could still hear her teacher's voice explaining the technique of painting light and dark, not as it is, but as we would represent it on the canvas.

Clair was suddenly suffused with the desire to paint, her entire body ached once again with the desire to be at work on a canvas. Was this a pleasure that was forbidden? How silly. She rejected the thought. Her mother had encouraged her to paint, sent Clair to art school instead of college when she asked for it. You've denied it to yourself, she chided. There's a canvas in the closet. You could go in and paint. But nothing was that simple. She knew she could start the canvas and then one of the children would need something, Paul would. . . Paul would what? Not want her, not now. He had barely spoken to her for weeks and now merely admitting him to consciousness made her restless, drove the thought, the desire to paint, back under the surface. She strode down the hill, anxiety making her careless, pushing her pace. She wanted to talk to someone. When Elizabeth came by now, they chatted, but did not talk. Clair felt none of the intimacy in their dialogue that had once satisfied her. She needed to talk. She needed to talk to a woman.

Striding down the path around the barn, she made up her mind. Clair got in her car and drove to Anna's.

"Remind me," said Clair, snuggling into a protected corner of Anna's porch and lifting her face to the sun, "remind me I have something to ask you. But let me bliss out on this sun first."

"Bliss out?" Anna cocked her head to one side, then sat next to Clair and handed her a coffee cup. "Clair, you've got to be kidding."

"It's Sharon. I think it's what the kids use to describe a new relationship. So and so are blissed out, she says."

"Good grief," Anna laughed, "it's California in Vermont."

They sat in silence for a moment, Anna looking speculatively at Clair, wondering as they sat there whether Clair knew about her fight – disagreement – with Elizabeth, wondering whether. . .

"I suppose," Clair said abruptly, turning to Anna, "you know what's been going on."

Anna raised one eyebrow. "Not really," she shrugged. Might as well start with it. "I haven't talked to Elizabeth for a couple of weeks, and it's been even longer," she smiled at Clair, "since I've seen you."

Clair was surprised and distressed. She had come to Anna because she assumed she would know where things stood between Paul and Elizabeth. What she really wanted to ask Anna was, so what's going to happen? Where is this going to leave me? And it seemed Anna might not know. In fact, she thought, looking at Anna more closely, Anna might not want to know. How could she have forgotten how Anna felt about Elizabeth, what she herself had assumed about their involvement? For a moment Clair felt confused, as though she had lost large chunks of her life and memory somewhere and had just tripped on something she had forgotten was there.

Anna waited for Clair to speak and when she didn't, she turned to her and said, "It's O.K. I think I know what you mean. We can talk about it if you want to."

Clair was still shaken by this betrayal of her memory, shaken by the intensity of her feelings as she faced the necessity of recounting to Anna the last few weeks.

"I'm really not sure what's happened myself," Clair admitted finally. "Paul goes around the house like. . ." she could not think of an analogy. "He's so morose." More than that, she needed to explain his behavior. She drew a deep breath. "I think he's having an affair with Elizabeth, but I don't understand. . ." She could not go on. Anna was looking at her sympathetically, then she lowered her eyes and looked away.

Oh, god, Anna thought, I guess it wasn't over between them. She had been sure that Elizabeth would not let this happen, sure of her loyalty to Clair, sure somehow that Elizabeth needed Clair more than she needed Paul.

"How do you know? I mean, what makes you think it?" Anna asked.

"It's Paul, I guess. He's sleeping on the sofa in the living room. He goes out in the car at all hours of the night without saying anything." She might as well tell it all. "He won't talk to me. When I speak to him, he ignores me or walks out of the house."

"Oh, jesus," Anna groaned, feeling immediately Clair's humiliation. "How could he do this to you? What do the children think?"

Clair shrugged. "He's clever. I don't think they really know what's happening. Just that something's weird." Clair paused, but had no energy to keep anything back. "In the past that's been my fault. I had a breakdown, you know." Anna was shaking her head, no. "Yeah, just before we came up here. Anyway, he talks to the kids. He takes them with him everywhere, like he's afraid to leave them with me or something." She sighed and turned her face to the sun again.

Anna wondered how much she should say, how much she could

say. Paul's behavior sounded crazed to her, but it was hard to know what was what.

"Look Clair, I know it's tough. But have you seen Elizabeth? Could you talk to her?"

Clair opened her eyes again. "Oh, I see her every other day or so."

"You do?" Anna's voice was slightly strained.

"Yeah. But I guess we've agreed not to talk about it." She thought back to that moment in her bedroom when she had accepted the tea and Elizabeth's concern and agreed to the silence between them, agreed by her compliance and her need to be what Elizabeth expected her to be. When they sat in the kitchen over coffee or tea, their talk would not have seemed that different to an outsider — news of the weather, the children, the animals. They no longer spoke of their men. And the deeper level of their conversations was missing, the substrata of emotion and caring that had nourished their friendship. Clair didn't love Elizabeth any less, but she felt constrained, like she could at any moment trip over a tree stump growing in the path of their every day conversation.

Anna did not know what to say. She was afraid of the rising level of anger and violence against Paul and Elizabeth that she felt in herself, felt grow and press hard on her stomach as she sat in apparent relaxation.

"I think it shits," Anna said with a suddenness that startled Clair. "I think they are both behaving despicably." She stood and walked out into the yard, picked up a branch lying in the grass and slapped it against her hand to emphasize her words.

Clair was alarmed at Anna's vehemence, then relieved. This was what she had come for, this confirmation of her own distress. She felt a rush of warmth toward Anna, who was sharing Clair's concern, her perspective.

Impulsively she said, "I know it must be hard for you, too."

Anna whirled toward her and faced Clair, her body rigid. "You do?" Her face contorted. "Did she tell you, too? Is there anyone in the county who doesn't know?"

Clair was shocked when Anna's anger and vehemence turned on her. She leaned back away from the force of this attack, not understanding it, thinking as she mentally backed away that she had been wrong to come here, wrong to try to share what was happening to her with someone else. It was her fault. She should not have come.

"I'm sorry," Anna's voice was low as she sat again on the porch and put her hand on Clair's knee. "I'm sorry," Anna said again, moved by the stricken look on Clair's face to explain further. "It's not that I'm ashamed that I love her. But I'm just beginning to figure all this out, and it's upsetting to think of her talking about it when I don't even know what it means."

"Who has she told?" Clair asked, surprised that this was what Anna meant.

"You mean she didn't tell you?" Anna looked intently at Clair again, then smiled, as if at a joke on herself. "You mean. . . ?" She was urging Clair to speak again, gently pulling her back into their conversation.

"I just assumed," Clair said awkwardly, not sure now why or what she had assumed. "I saw you cared for her," she twisted her coffee cup anxiously, turning it around and around between her hands, willing herself not to make another mistake. "Who did she tell?" she asked, knowing before she finished the question.

"Paul." Anna's voice was quiet and for a moment there was silence between them. They sat in the sun, Anna leaning back now, Clair forward, staring at the wet bark on the old maple beside the porch.

Anna sat up with a sigh. "What will you do?"

"Do?" Clair sounded surprised, remembered that this was what she'd come to ask Anna.

"Will you leave him? You can't stay, can you?"

"Leave him?" Stupid, Clair berated herself. Stop sounding like an echo. With an effort she brought her attention to focus on what Anna asked. Leave him? Could she do that? What about the children, think of the children. The inner voice spoke to her, controlling, remember what you and Paul said about Elizabeth taking the children away from their father?

"I don't think I could leave him. It wouldn't be fair to the children," her voice was rote, self-righteous.

Anna looked at her sideways. "Yes, well, there is that."

"I never wanted children," Clair's words came out of her as though each was being torn separately from her larynx. She felt the gall and bitterness of years rise, the strength of these feelings making her dizzy. She rocked forward, clasping her hands around her knees. Something inside her was letting go and she did not think she could afford to let it happen, but did not know how to stop it. She felt the tears begin and thought, I can't cry, I can't let him do this to me again. But the tears came anyway and the words, "I never wanted children, I never wanted children," over and over as she cried and sat on Anna's porch and rocked and rocked.

Moved and alarmed, Anna sat next to her. She had nothing to say, no words of advice, direction or counsel, no experience to guide her. So she just sat next to Clair, her arm around the other woman as she cried.

When Clair began to grow quiet, she could feel Anna's arm, heavy around her shoulders. "Hey, are you O.K. now?" Anna asked, nothing in her voice reproaching Clair.

"Yeah," Clair gulped the word. Then breathed deeply. "God, how embarrassing." She wanted to look away from Anna.

"I'd say you've been under a strain. I don't see why it's embarrassing."

Clair pulled a kleenex out of her jacket pocket and blew her nose. "I guess I have been under some strain," she admitted, as though this were a new idea to her. Then, still feeling her embarrassment, she rose from the porch. "I guess I'd better get back."

Anna watched her stand, but made no move to stop her. "You can come back anytime," she said.

Clair drove out the long driveway, negotiating the spring potholes and mud ruts. At the top of the hill she pulled the car over to the side of the road and sat looking down at the grey purple mountain range rising up as far as she could see. There was something she wanted to remember, something in what just happened that she knew she needed to hold onto, re-examine and test. Her eye wandered to the rows of apple trees stretching off to her left. The buds were swollen, but had not yet broken into leaf, giving the branches a nobby, gnarled look. As though they were over-used, Clair thought, looking at the heavy bent branches.

It was not really that she had not wanted children, she insisted now to herself. She didn't hate or dislike her daughters, indeed, she loved them, cherished each in her differentness and difficulty. But she had *wanted* something else with the passionate connection that other women seemed to want their children. She wanted something else, but she had the chidren and made them do, suffice. Now she knew that if she — they — were going to survive, she would have to find the something else.

There was more. She pushed herself back into the memory of those moments on the porch, bringing back the fear, feeling the tears rise again for a moment. Then she knew. I can't cry. I can't let him do this to me again. Paul was doing this to her. But only if she let him. That was what she must hold onto. That was what she needed to know. I won't let him do this to me. She said it over and over to herself as she started the car again.

Paul and the girls were unloading the groceries when she drove in. He looked at her with surprise and she knew he was wondering where she had been, so seldom did she go out alone. Clair waved with deliberate cheerfulness, zipped the car into her parking spot and slammed the door.

"Hi. How was town?" she asked cheerfully of no one in particular.

Paul looked at her doubtfully, hefted a bag of groceries in each arm and headed into the kitchen without answering her.

"Fine, Mom," said Tammie, obviously embarrased by Paul's silence, ready to duck into the kitchen herself. Clair picked up a bag of groceries and followed them. She wondered if he had been talking to the girls and, if he had, what he had said. But, she admitted, he might have said nothing. Their awkwardness might come out of the silences in the house, for she knew that they would not have forgotten what happened the last time this strained, unnatural silence came upon them.

Paul and Sharon brought in the last two bags and set them on the counter. "I could use some help up in the barn," Paul said, inclining his head toward the two children. "I'll drive the truck up and we'll unload the feed bags." He turned toward the door and Tammie and Sharon started to follow him, unprotesting.

Clair stood in the middle of the kitchen, surrounded by the week's supply of groceries, and wondered whether she should speak or remain silent and enjoy the solitude while she unpacked, sorted, shelved. She remembered her resolve in the car and decided to speak.

"It's Tammie's day for the kitchen. She can help me unpack and then come up to you." She stood, waiting to see if anyone would hear her.

Paul looked surprised again, then gave Tammie a significant look. "You heard your mother."

Tammie looked scared, Clair thought. "Sure, Mom," she said and began to unpack a grocery bag. Clair worked with her, chatting quietly, trying to create an aura of normalcy in the everydayness of their words and work. For a while Tammie became her ten year old self, clowning, joking about the mean clerk at the Agway feed store, balancing three rolls of paper towels on her head as she pirouetted around the kitchen.

When they finished, Clair sent her up to help with the feed and watched from the kitchen window as this child of hers bounded up the hill, filled with spring, the sun, the day of release from school routine. As Tammie approached the barn, she leaped to the top of a stone wall, part of an old foundation, swung her arms exuberantly, then pounded her chest, a mocking king of all she surveyed. Clair laughed out loud in the silent kitchen. She turned back to the chickens she was cutting up to put in the freezer, reflecting ruefully that Tammie's jeans were three inches short at the ankle and she hadn't even worn them out yet. As she sliced and chopped the chickens, pulled the wingbone out of the socket and then pressed the knife through flesh and cartilage, she tried to think calmly about what she owed these children, what they needed from her, how much they expected from her and what she could give.

She dumped the last piece of chicken into the plastic bag. As she pushed the bags into the meat side of the freezer, she saw the remnants of last summer's vegetables grown in the garden, picked, blanched, frozen now, so green and yellow, waiting to be eaten. She really should get out the potting soil and start some new plants for the garden, she told herself as she shut the freezer door. Then she remembered. She remembered Paul and she remembered being on the porch with Anna. And Clair decided she would not take the bag of potting soil out from under the sink. To start a garden now would commit her to a future in which she did not believe. Instead she walked back to the small room off the kitchen where her paints and sewing machine were kept. For a moment she surveyed the mess of material, dust and disorder, and then began to sort through her tubes of paint.

# Chapter 12

Elizabeth carried the lunch bowls from the kitchen table to the sink and rinsed and stacked them. She noticed that the old chipped porcelain sink was filthy again, but didn't bother to run the sponge around it. It would take a more serious effort. Everything about this old farm house required serious effort, although she never said anything to Tom about it. He grew up in the house and so had his father, each of them in his turn maintaining what was there, disdaining the modernizations which city folk like Paul and Clair insisted on before they would farm. Elizabeth often envied Clair her remodeled kitchen, the smooth countertops that weren't hard to clean, the dishwasher, the new range and freezer, all of those things which seemed so unnecessary to a man like Tom who seldom spent time in the house at all, much less the kitchen. Elizabeth had often heard him tell of growing up without indoor plumbing, and as she rinsed the loose crumbs down the drain, she wondered what it must have been like for Tom's mother to carry water in from the pump to this very sink. She would have had to heat it, too, for the hot water heater which stood against the kitchen wall was installed less than twenty years ago. She was sure it had been Tom's mother who had finally insisted on indoor plumbing, just as she, Elizabeth, wanted to insist on making some changes. Tom liked things the way they were. She knew she would have to deal with that. He liked their relationship just as it was, but Elizabeth knew she was going to have to get him to change his mind about that, too.

She pushed open the kitchen door and went out into the yard where Tom and all five children were hammering and shouting. Anna had called midweek and told Elizabeth she thought she would take the job in Oregon, leaving as soon as the semester was over. She was calling to ask if Pam would like to have Rose when Anna left. She couldn't transport a fat, twenty year old horse all the way to Oregon, and what did Elizabeth think? Could they afford it? Would Pam want her, or would Rose just be something else for Elizabeth to take care of?

Elizabeth didn't have to consider. "Why don't you ask Pam yourself," she said. And for days now, Pam blissfully counted the hours left until May 5th when Anna would ride Rose over to their barn.

With three weeks left until delivery day, Pam thought there was barely enough time to do all of the things required for such an event. She had pestered Tom from the moment he got home on Friday night about where they could build a horse stall in the barn. All morning Elizabeth checked their progress as she moved in and out of the house with feed for the geese and chickens, hung one load of wash and then another, and marveled at her eleven year old general who was giving directions, wielding a hammer, designing a box stall as though she had done it a dozen times before. And she watched Tom comply good naturedly with each of Pam's demands.

"Now, Tom, I want you to hold this end and, Larry, you hold right down here." Pam's blond hair was tucked behind each ear and she wore a riding cap plunked down securely over her forehead.

My god, Elizabeth laughed to herself, she's even got Larry working on it. Pam hammered the board into place and stepped back to survey her work, reached into her jeans pocket for another nail and went back at it.

"Jees, don't you think that's enough," Larry started to complain. "It's not like you're getting the black stallion, it's just old Rose."

"Rose is not old," Pam stepped back, her hands on her hips, surveying Larry with a school teacher's look. "A horse is in its prime at twenty. Horses live a long time, not like dogs," she made the word dog sound slightly scornful.

"That's right," echoed Shanna reverently, following Pam's every move and gesture, "horses live a long time." She stood so close to Pam that she had to move whenever Pam stepped backward. She watched Pam with worshipful eyes. Elizabeth could see that soon one horse would not be enough.

"What do you think?" Tom asked. "Is it taking shape?"

"It looks wonderful." She turned to Pam. "Are you going to close it in or will it be a tie stall?"

"Well," Pam began importantly, "Anna uses a tie stall and it is what she's used to." Then she confessed, "I don't think I know how to make a gate, Mom."

Elizabeth laughed. "I don't think you need one, sweetheart." She crossed to where Tom was still holding up his end of the board and put her arms around him from behind.

"Thanks for helping," she said, rubbing her face in his back.

"Hey, what's guy to do?" he asked. "This is important stuff." Then he grinned around at her. "But you could hold this board for a while. I want to start the old tractor and take a look out at the back fields."

Elizabeth traded places with him while Pam went on with her hammering. She wondered why he wanted to take the tractor out, but didn't ask. She was planning the rest of the afternoon and the evening mentally, running a dozen possible scenarios by, shifting and selecting, trying to anticipate and shape Tom's response to what she was going to tell him.

She had walked out of the doctor's office Friday afternoon, dazed, still unwilling to believe that she was pregnant again. She had been using an IUD since Artie was born and when she missed one period, she hadn't thought anything of it, assumed she was tired, stressed by winter. The second miss worried her, but again she thought it must be the IUD or some minor abnormality. She even wondered about menopause, but dismissed that – she was too young, that just wasn't possible for her yet. She walked into the doctor's office in a casual mood, carting Colin and Artie, joking with the office nurses.

"Mom, you're letting that board slip," Pam's protesting voice brought her back to the present. "It's got to be exactly straight, you know." She held her hands on her hips again, head cocked to one side in frustration.

"Sorry, boss," Elizabeth was contrite, lining her long board up with the others. Larry had slipped out when Tom left. By craning her neck, she could see out of the barn door without letting go of her board. There he was, holding on to the seat of the tractor, bouncing out to the back fields wih Tom. Shanna, Colin and Artie were playing in the dirt barnyard, a game that had something to do with the lines Shanna was drawing in the dirt with one of Pam's nails. The two goslings, young geese now, strutted around, in and out, between the children, their necks pushing forward with each step. Matilda still wouldn't let these strangers in the goose pen, and so Elizabeth kept them in a separate cage on the back porch at night. Nothing is ever simple, she sighed, her thoughts returning to herself, to the children, to Tom.

"Mom," Shanna's voice, a high shriek, interrupted her. "Simon and Garfunkle are walking in my game. They're messing up the lines."

"Go get a scoop of feed and put it in the corner of the barn here," Elizabeth suggested, keeping her voice calm and helpful in spite of her rising inner irritation. Five children was enough, she knew that, especially when the responsibility for them rested solely with her. Enough is enough, she repeated again, cursing the mechanical failure, her own body's will to impregnate. The doctor mentioned her options, avoiding any reference about what he knew of her personal life, that she was not living wih her husband, that the divorce would not be final for another three months, that custody of her children was dependent, in part, upon Edward's good will. Everyone in the village knew these things, Elizabeth was sure. When she left the office, she could hear his voice suggesting that there were two more weeks left in her first term, and she should think about what this would mean to her.

What it meant made her slightly dizzy every time she thought about it. She helped Pam straighten a bent nail, waited while she tried to hammer it, helped her straighten it again, sighed with relief as it went in.

"That looks wonderful, Pam. I think you're done, don't you?" She hoped it was done.

Pam pushed her hat back on her forehead and looked around, satisfied with what she could see. "Do you think she'll like it, Mom?"

"I think she'll love it," Elizabeth made her voice enthusiastic, wondering as she did so how she would fit yet another animal into her routine. "You know what? Next time Anna comes over you can show it to her and see what she thinks. How about that?"

Pam nodded, pleased, and walked around the interior of the stall once again. Elizabeth could see she was not ready to leave.

"I'll get the eggs for you, if you want," she offered.

"Thanks, Mom." Pam barely looked toward her. She was contemplating the front of the stall. "I just want to fix this tie-up."

Elizabeth took a bucket down from a hook and walked out into the barnyard and around to the chicken coop. She stooped to enter the low shed, still warm from the afternoon sun. The strong odor of chicken shit mingled with the musty smell of winter feathers. Elizabeth wondered, as she moved from nest to nest, how she could explain – to herself first, then Tom – why she could not have an abortion.

It was the sensible thing to do, one voice argued. You've done O.K. with five children, kept your youth, your body, why tempt fate? Remember your mother? How tired she always was? But I'm different, Elizabeth argued back. Mother must have been sick. She died so young. I'm healthy. I'm in good shape. Elizabeth was proud of her body, proud of her slimness and strength, still proud of the way her muscles had come taut again after each of the babies. She could manage one more. And then she would have something permanent done, she promised herself. No more mechanical failures.

There was just one thing she wanted, one empty feeling right in her center, as she was carried forward by the adrenalin of this crisis. She wanted to talk to someone about this.

"Hey old girl, move over just a little, that's it, that's it," she crooned to the hens, her voice a soporific, soothing the hens into compliance.

She sighed and straightened her stooped back. She was going to talk to Tom tonight, wasn't she? No. She took it back. She was going to tell Tom tonight. What she missed was someone with whom she could talk.

She ducked under the door sill of the chicken coop and sat for a moment on the low step, hidden from the activity around the corner of the barnyard. She felt deserted by Anna and Clair. Surely, she thought, Clair could see by now that Elizabeth was not going to take Paul away, and, yet, each time she stopped in, Clair seeemed more distant, more withdrawn, until Elizabeth barely had the patience to stop by. And Anna. She stopped herself. She did not want to think about Anna. Tonight she would tell Tom that she was carrying his child.

Back in the barnyard she picked Artie up in her free arm to carry him into the kitchen with her. She paused in the barn door to check on Pam and saw her oldest child had pulled down a bale of hay, opened it, and was now spreading the fresh hay on the stall floor, humming to herself as she pulled apart each sheaf and patted it into place. Elizabeth shook her head, but did not interrupt. She did not have to tell Pam now that the barn floor was damp and the hay would mold long before Anna delivered Rose. Elizabeth went into the kitchen to prepare supper.

After dinner and dishes and baths for all five children, Elizabeth walked slowly down the back stairs of the old house into the kitchen again. She was tired, more angry and impatient with the children than she ever could remember herself being. Larry dawdling in the bath, running the faucets after she had opened the drain, whining about the cold when she yanked him out of the tub — it all seemed to try her past exhaustion. The difuse anger that had flickered at the edges of her peripheral vision threatened to focus on any object in her path as she came closer and closer to her talk with Tom. It isn't fair, it isn't fair, was the angry echo in her mind as she catalogued her grievances. She didn't deserve this pregnancy. Why had Anna deserted her just now? And Clair? Clair seemed to be fading further and further from Elizabeth, receding into a background in which their intimacy had never existed.

She went to the cupboard and pulled out two glasses and a small bottle of brandy she had bought on the way home from the doctor. Another level of emotion began to settle over Elizabeth's shoulders and back, firming the stress points in her shoulder blades. She was too intent on what was before her to recognize the despair for what it was. I'm tired, she told herself.

Tom was stretched out on the sofa when she walked into the living room, not sound asleep, but dozing. A small fire burned on the hearth to take the chill out of the April evening, and Elizabeth settled gratefully into the chair next to him. She sat the brandy and glasses on the table in front of her and poured two glasses, picked hers up and settled back into her chair with a sigh. Next to her, Tom's nose twitched and one eye opened.

"Mmmmrrumph."

"That's right."

"Mmmm?"

"Brandy," she waved the snifter closer to his nose.

"What's the occasion?" Both eyes were open now and, as was characteristic of him, he went directly to the point. He reached for his glass and swirled the liquor around, reflecting the light of the fire off his glass.

Elizabeth laughed briefly and tried to keep her voice light as she raised her glass in a toast. "Here's to spring."

"Yeah," Tom swung his feet to the ground and sat up, raising his glass to touch hers. "It was a nice day. That Pam is sure excited about getting an old nag."

"Now you heard what she said, " Elizabeth's voice was mocking, gentle. "Rose is in her prime."

Tom grunted assent, then looked over at Elizabeth. She could see that, although he would not ask her again, he was still waiting for her to explain.

"I guess I really do have an announcement."

He nodded, waited for her to continue.

She began with the disclaimers, nervous again in spite of herself. "This doesn't have to mean anything about our relationship, I mean, I'm not telling you this to lay extra responsibility on you or anything, Tom. I mean, I can cope with it by myself, it really shouldn't have to affect us," she paused. She could see he was doubtful, not understanding what she was aiming at, looking a little glum; for he was intelligent enough to know that her disclaimers of change meant that she was proposing a change, and he had just begun to feel comfortable. She sighed and began again.

"I went to the doctor yesterday." Now Tom sat up straight, but still did not question her. "He said I'm pregnant." There. She said it.

"What?" He was surprised. She could see that, but she could not tell yet how the news was affecting him.

"I'm pregnant."

"I heard you. How can you be pregnant? I thought you were taking care of that? I didn't think you could get pregnant." He was slightly self righteous now, as though he were accused of something.

"I was, I am," Elizabeth was soothing now, gentling down the irritation like she smoothed the wrinkles out of the laundry as she folded it. "He said it was extraordinary, it shouldn't have happened." She tried a small irony, "He said we must be impossibly fertile."

Tom grunted again, looking into the fire, not at her. She watched his long, loose jointed fingers wrap themselves around and around the glass. Then he finished the brandy in a single swallow.

"Well, I guess we can get an abortion." He looked at her to see if that was what she was meaning.

Elizabeth thought for a moment. She poured a little more brandy in each of their glasses and went to sit next to him on the couch, snuggling up against his side, bringing up her knees and feet.

"I know that would be the rational thing to do." She ran the back of her hand down his cheek, soothing, petting. "But I don't think I can. I want this baby, Tom. Even if it is a big family already."

For that moment she did want the baby, wanted the security of this bond which would surely tie Tom to her. But in the next instant, she also wanted the opposite. She wanted to go back in time, not to be pregnant, to feel free and in control, able to take what she wanted from Tom and still feel she could come and go as she liked. The snares she was setting, she knew, would bind them both.

Tom settled back now on the sofa and laid his arm heavily over her shoulder . "Hmmpf," he said, half smiling at the fire. Then he stretched his legs out in front of him and turned to Elizabeth. "Well, I had a look at the back pasture today."

Elizabeth refrained from shaking her head in disbelief, wondering how he had leaped from her pregnancy to the back pasture.

"I know," she said. "I watched you and Larry sneak away from the stall project. I got left holding the board." She laughed tentatively.

"Mmm. Don't you want to know why I was out there?" He was smiling now, but she could not quite read the tone of the smile.

"Of course I want to know."

"Well, I thought I might re-seed and hay it this year."

"Just because we're getting one horse?" Elizabeth's voice rose in disbelief.

Tom laughed out loud. "I've been thinking of reactivating the farm. I want to farm. Always have. Couldn't do it by myself. And there were so many debts when Dad died. But I held onto all the land. Paul's leasing some of it, but it's still there. We could start with a few heifers this fall, plant it all next summer and have most of a herd about a year and a half from now." He settled his head back against the cushions, looking pleased, waiting for her response.

Well, well, thought Elizabeth, surprised. Fancy Tom having his own agenda. She wondered how long he'd been thinking over all of this, mulling it in private. She wondered if he would have dared to bring it up himself if she had not — not what? — committed herself to this relationship with him. Yes, that was what she was doing. He was thinking she would stay now, she saw, as he turned and took her hand and spoke again.

"I never thought you'd stay with me." His voice was gentle, but she thought she could hear the ring of victory in his soft tones. "I thought you were just stopping here on your way to someplace else."

Elizabeth looked at the handsome, serious, large-boned face so close to her own. That was what I intended, she thought but could not say, and the realization weighted her whole body. She felt as though she had been jerked forward in a car in which the brakes were suddenly slammed on. She sighed, willing herself with every last bit of energy to retrieve something for herself from all of this, some portion of who she was when she came to him. She wanted to remember the Elizabeth who could walk out on Edward, bundle five children in a car and just leave.

"Well," she said, forcing her voice into humor, "I wasn't exactly travelling lightly when you met me. Stopping here was more like the invasion of a mad army, wasn't it?" And would that we will be able to fold our tents and disappear again in the night if we have to, she added in a silent promise.

"I'm used to family," Tom said.

Elizabeth nodded.

"We'll get married, then." He was not asking a question.

She nodded again. Yes, that was inevitable, she supposed. But there need be nothing permanent about a marriage, she knew that. Elizabeth poured a third brandy, dulling the voice of protest that seemed to be wailing inside her, wailing against the pretension she was trying to build for herself that everything was fine. She could cope, this had turned out well, better than she had expected. She could cope with things now, she knew she could cope.

Beside her, she could feel Tom's pleasure. When she started to pour from the brandy bottle again, he took the brandy glass away.

"Let's go up to bed," he said, pushing the fire to the back of the hearth and fitting the screen around it. Elizabeth was too tired to protest.

Mounting the stairs to bed, she hoped that this would make things seem simpler. She would know what to expect from people. She would know what to do.

She walked into the bedroom, stepping over the jeans and shirt Tom had let drop on the floor. She unbuttoned her shirt without looking at the bed, then slid out of her jeans. She ran the hairbrush through her hair and leaned over the dresser, looking at her face in the mirror. Her own ice-blue eyes looked out at her, large and apparently serene over the high cheekbones, weathered and slightly flushed from the sun and brandy. She sighed. There were no answers in the mirror. She turned toward the bed.

# Chapter 13

Clair was packing. She did not know at first, as she went from room to room, sorting, stacking, dusting, opening the storm windows and lowering the screens, that she was packing. Spring house cleaning was what she had called it for years. This year she began in the living room where Paul had been sleeping for several weeks. She circled the couch as she orbited the room, vacuuming cobwebs from above the hearth and last winter's cluster flies from between the window pane and sill. She took the oval braid colonial rug out to the line and struggled to pull it over by herself, getting it finally, panting, straightening the folds out so that it hung free in the spring breeze. Tammie and Sharon would take turns thwacking it with an old broom when they came home from school, sneezing as the dust filtered out from among the braids. Then she mopped the floor, polished the furniture, and sorted through the brickabrack of the eighteen years of her life with Paul. The small Hummel figurine of a girlchild standing next to a goose, she dusted and returned to the mantle. Paul had bought it for them on their first trip to Europe. But when she dusted the dark mahogany head of an African woman, carved with a nose following straight from the forehead, firm lips jutting, Clair slipped this piece into the large pocket of the canvas apron she was wearing and did not take it out again until she wandered back to her sewing room where she put it carefully in a box next to one of her palettes. She never cared much for European representational art, she thought, as she walked by the Hummel. Finally approaching the couch, she pulled the stuffed pillows away from the frame and carried them out to the lawn, to the fresh green grass, where she spread them in the sun and began to pound them with the broom. Dust rose glittering in the light.

So it had gone, room to room, one or two small objects finding their way into Clair's apron pocket: a book from the hall shelves, an antique cup of her mother's from the dining room china cabinet, a sketch of Sharon's, done when she was eight that Clair had framed and hung. At first she was just straightening, and that happened, too; the piles of debris and treasures needed to be sorted through. Though she forced the realization away from consciousness for a while, she could not help but be aware of how little there was in this house that was hers, that she cared for or even liked. The furniture, for instance, was Paul's choice. It was tasteful, expensive, comfortable, suited to his New Jersey image of a successful man. She could not even describe it further, supposing it some blend of Danish and American Business.

When she finally stood in her sewing room after two weeks of cleaning and sorting and found herself wondering if the sewing machine would fit into the back of her car, Clair started to laugh, then caught the back of her hand in her mouth, fearful, strained, surprised. But how could you be surprised, she wondered, for she had been planning to leave Paul – and leave the children – since that day she sat in the orchard on Anna's porch.

But she did not know how to do it. She was locked into a routine, into the daily expectations of her children, the needs of the farm, and even of Paul. He spoke to her occasionally now, gently and simply as one speaks to a child or a patient recovering in the hospital. He seemed to be gazing down at Clair from unimaginable heights, gazing at her in mild bemusement and some worry, the doctor looking at a patient who does not understand her symptoms. She did not know if he saw her packing, if he knew that was what she was doing. All her paints were sorted into boxes, a few empty canvases rolled and stacked. She even put some clothes into a small case and brought it down to her sewing room where all of the boxes were neatly arranged. She wanted none of the paintings hanging on the wall; she felt them to be fake, forgeries out of a past she never lived.

She was ready to start again, but she had no money of her own. She had no destination. And so she stayed, day after day, with all of her possessions packed and ready. Clair marked time, walked in place, trod forward on the routine of breakfast, lunch, dinner, without ever going anywhere. Time was not even passing, she felt, although the month grew greener and greener, the days longer and the air warmer.

"I plowed the garden for you last week," Paul said, standing directly in front of Clair as she moved from stove to kitchen table, her hands filled with two laden soup bowls which she shoved toward him when he stopped her.

"Don't you think," he continued, taking the bowls, but reluctant to let her go, "you ought to be planting. I mean," he set the bowls in front of Tammie and Sharon and sat down at the table himself, waiting for her to return with his soup, "don't you usually start things indoors?"

He waved toward the south window, lined with shelves for plants, nearly empty now. Clair ladled two more bowls of soup without answering and turned toward the table.

When she set Paul's soup down in front of him, she said, without looking at him, "You can't plant yet. You can't plant until Good Friday up here." She paused and walked to her place at the opposite end of the table. "And I thought I might not have a garden this year."

"What do you mean?" His voice was sharp, angry. "I thought you liked gardening." Then without waiting for her to answer, "Are you feeling all right? What's wrong with you?"

It was the first time he had said anything like this in front of the children, and Clair saw Sharon give Tammie a significant look across the soup bowl which the younger girl tried to ignore, keeping her eyes cast down toward her chicken and noodles.

"Nothing is wrong with me, Paul," Clair insisted, her voice firm and calm. "Yes, I like gardening, but it's a lot of work and," she paused, considered the lie, then went forward, "besides, we don't need a garden this year." She smiled at Tammie. "Pass me the salt, please."

"Sure, Mom," she gulped the words, then returned to her soup, trying to finish and get away from the table.

"What do you mean, we don't need a garden?" Paul was sarcastic. "Are we going to eat hay like the cows?" Sharon giggled nervously at the tension rising from the center of the table.

"We still have vegetables left in the freezer from last year and from the year before."

She knew Paul had never looked in the freezer, wouldn't know she spoke a half truth, a lie really, she corrected herself. There were some vegetables left, a few gaunt broccoli stems from the first garden, lots of bags of useless zucchini from last year, but even if Paul got up from the table now and challenged her by opening the freezer and looking, he wouldn't be able to tell what was there.

She smiled across the table at him. "We really ought to eat what's there. And when the weather is a little warmer, Sharon can plant some lettuce and cucumbers for salads. That's all we need."

Defeated, Paul finished his soup, but could not resist a retort as he stood to leave the table. "You could have at least told me this before I plowed the whole garden."

Clair's anger rose to match his for a moment. "You could have asked me if I wanted the garden plowed, Paul." Her anger flared, then snuffed out quickly like a match, leaving the smell of sulphur lingering in the air, distinct, dangerous.

As she moved from table to sink, sink to table, the repetition of meaningless chores seemed at last to slow Clair. She felt the blood in her arms and legs congeal, as she lost the flow of habit. She had to think about each task, each movement as she made herself perform it. Lift the plate, slide the saltines back into the tin canister, replace the lid, rinse the crumbs off the plate, stack the plate in the dishwasher. It was finally, too much. She left the children's soup bowls sitting where they had left them and climbed slowly up to her bedroom to lie down.

The fear of danger, the imminence of explosion, climbed the stairs with her and lay down across the bed. Her nervousness was in the lethargy she could not seem to shake off: her fear, palpable and ugly, lying beside her, was that she would not escape.

"How can I go away?" she had asked Anna on a second visit, the urgency of having discovered that she was packing still new within her.

They walked through the greening orchard, now fast, now slow, the pace of their talk driving them.

"What do you mean, how?" Anna asked, her eyes narrowing as she and Clair turned down another row of trees, walked facing into the setting sun. "Do you mean how can you justify it?"

"No. I mean where would I go? How would I live?" She kicked angrily at a branch on the ground that had been pruned from one of the young trees they were walking by. "I've never had a job. I wouldn't know how to begin to find one, or what I could do."

Anna was thoughtful, silent. She could not remember a time in her life since she was thirteen when she had not been working at a job for a wage. It had been part of her parents' careful preparation for her, not dire necessity, that sent her out to work. But gradually her skills and her expectation of her own competence made her self reliant.

"And if I just left — with no money, no job — they'd say I was mad again." There. It was out. That was her fear, expressed for the first time, never far away from her.

Anna walked on in silence for another moment, her hands shoved deep in her pockets. "You know what Emily Dickinson says about that?" Clair shook her head negatively. " 'Much madness is divinest sense?' " Anna's voice rose in a question and Clair nodded, she did remember something of it.

"What's the rest of it?" she asked.

" 'Assent, and you are sane, demur, you're straightway dangerous, and handled with a chain.' You know — like to be normal you have to be like everybody else, do what every one expects you to do."

They stood at the top of the hill and looked down at the lake, deep blue-black in the incipient twilight.

"Look, Clair," Anna turned and faced the smaller woman who stood beside her, who seemed so fragile next to the rough and twisted branches of the trees all around them. How to say it gently, she wondered? "Look, maybe it's none of my business, but," she sighed and the words came quickly, "Paul's not poor. I know it takes money to run a farm. But he has money, money for any project he wants to try. You have money. It belongs to you, too, it has to, you've worked with Paul for years. He owes you something, O.K.? He owes you."

He owes you, he owes you, echoed now as Clair lay on the bed, gathering her energy to go down and begin the preparation for supper. He may owe me, she thought bitterly, but being owed and collecting are two different things, that's for sure.

She heard Tom's car drive in while she was fixing dinner, turned a moment from the stove to check and see if Elizabeth and the children were with him, but he was alone. He climbed up to the barn where Paul was milking. When he left she heard the car again, and was relieved he hadn't stopped in to see her.

Around six she glanced up to the barn to see if Paul was finished. The light in the milking parlor was off and, at first, she could not see him. Then he moved and she caught sight of him. He was standing in the shadow of the barn watching the sun fade over the western hill opposite. He stood and stood and Clair decided not to call the children down to dinner yet. She would wait until Paul came in.

By seven o'clock the last rose streak was fading from the sky and Clair was about to call Tammie to go and fetch Paul when she heard him on the porch, taking off his barn boots. He opened the door slowly and when she looked at him he seemed very old and tired.

"Well," his voice was sarcastic, biting, blaming her. "I suppose you've heard the good news?" He went to the whiskey bottle under the sink, pulled it out, poured a shot glass and left the bottle on the counter.

"News?" Clair tensed. His entire voice and attitude toward her had changed. She was no longer the child or the patient.

"The *good* news." He raised his glass in a toast.

Clair waited.

"Well, well. You don't know?" His head to one side, Paul contemplated her. "Come on, then. Guess." He was sneering.

Clair shrugged, then turned to the stove. "I wouldn't know where to begin. Are you ready to eat?"

"They're getting married."

Clair stopped in her reach for the frying pan, the lid suspended in mid-air from one hand, the spatula from the other. Tom. That was what he had wanted. For a moment she felt relief. Now things could go back to normal. Paul would behave. Things could go on as they were. She was relieved, for a moment, and in that moment stood at the stove and remembered wth pleasure the morning they had all been in the kitchen together during the winter, that moment she so carefully stored to remember at a time like this to pull her back into the pleasures of this life; that moment when the fire seemed most bright and cheerful, the color and smells of the kitchen most vivid, the company most pleasant and satisfying. They could go back now, she thought as she stood at the stove, to a normal life. And then her hand started to shake and her breath seemed to rush out of her body. Go back? She could never go back to what had been before. Wasn't she already packed to leave?

The pan lid clunked back down on the pan and she turned to look at Paul, holding the spatula defensively in front of her. She could think of nothing to say.

They stood for a moment like that and then Paul broke the silence.

"Well, I suppose you're pleased." He drained his glass and walked over to the counter to pour another.

"Well, surprised. When did they decide?" Clair tried to keep her voice within a normal range.

Paul shrugged. "He wants the lower acreage back. He says I can plant it this year, but he wants it back next spring."

"They're going to farm?" Clair was surprised. She only thought of Tom as the salesman, traveling around the state, drinking, finding new women. This would be much better for Elizabeth. Perhaps, she thought, it is what Elizabeth wanted. But she had to ask. "Why are they doing it?"

"What? Farming?"

"Why are they getting married?" Her question was firm.

"He knocked her up, why else?"

She could see Paul watching for her response to this announcement, but could not withhold the frown of concern. Elizabeth always seemed so in control to Clair. How could this ever happen? How had Elizabeth let this happen, she corrected herself? For surely there were other choices and she was chosing to marry Tom and have this child.

"It's not my kid," Paul interrupted her thoughts, beligerant and sneering again.

Clair raised her head sharply, her wide-set brown eyes looked directly into Paul's eyes for the first time in weeks. There it was, the thing that had been between them, out in the open for the first time, almost palpable, suspended in the tension that ran from one to the other. It was in the open. She had permission to talk about it. But with that permission, Clair realized she did not know what she wanted to say. She needed time to think, to plan.

"Call the children, Paul. Dinner is ready." He dropped his eyes and obeyed.

She chatted lightly through dinner with the children. Paul maintained a sullen, brooding silence at his end of the table, getting up once to refill his glass. If the children noticed, they said nothing. Clair and Tammie and Sharon talked about the new clutch of chicks, talked with the firm intention of ignoring Paul's obvious displeasure at the other end of the table.

Why? That was the question she wanted to ask most. Not why did you do it, but why did you do this to me, treat me this way while you were doing it? Why did it have to be my fault that things in the house weren't normal? And yet, Clair wasn't sure that she wanted to talk about it at all, so accustomed was she to the silences between them, the silences that seemed safe compared to her anger at lunch, the smell of danger that had lingered even as she lay resting on the bed. But the silence had been smothering her, she knew that, too, and now she must choose between the smothering and the spark of her anger.

As she loaded the dishwasher, counting it perhaps the millionth time she had loaded it, she realized she had thought Paul would make this choice for her, by making it impossible for her to stay. She thought he meant to drive her out of the house so that he could bring Elizabeth in, and in part, she was willing to acquiesce to his petulance, his long silence, his obvious punishment of her, because it meant she could leave, that he gave her permission to leave. But Elizabeth was marrying Tom. What would Paul want from her now?

They maintained silence and distance during the evening hours until the children both went up to bed. Paul sat in the living room, a book on his lap which he did not even bother to open, and stared at the immaculate fireplace hearth Clair had cleaned during the week. Clair stayed in the kitchen and her sewing room until she heard Sharon's steps going up, the slow methodical trod of feet reluctant to depart. She knows something's happening, Clair thought. Now she could hear Paul get up from his chair and come back out to the whiskey bottle, pour, wander for a moment around the kitchen. She knew he was looking for her, knew also that he would not come into "her" room to find her. It was time to go out and face him. Clair's hands gripped the sewing table, her knuckles whitening under pressure. What do I want, she asked, surveying this small room to which she had brought everything from her life that held meaning for her, what do I want? Could she face his anger, stand against his accusations, not let him convince her that she had been wrong, done something wrong? She turned and faced the door, walked out through the kitchen and into the living room.

Paul was crying. She stopped, staring. He sat slumped over in the large chair, head in his hands, sobbing like a child bereft. She was shocked. She felt the tides of habit and old affection pour into her like adrenalin, willing her to move toward him, embrace him, wrap his wound in her arms, heal him and comfort him, make him whole again by taking his burden upon herself. But she could not move forward. Something else rooted her feet, tied her arms, made her jaw rigid. She stood, unable to go forward or back.

"God, oh, god," his sobs were becoming articulate now, he knew she was in the room. "Oh, god, I feel so awful." It was a moan, a complaint.

Clair crossed to her chair and sat down next to him, still unable to speak. She was looking at him almost curiously, unable to remember ever seeing him like this. He had never cried, not once in the eighteen years they had lived together. Should she ask him what was wrong? Clair supposed there were things she ought to be saying, doing, but she could not think what they were.

"What's wrong, Paul?"

"It's such a mess," he did not raise his head, but seemed glad she had spoken. "I don't know what happened, I don't know how it happened."

Clair's head was to one side again, contemplating him with a speculative look.

"I'm sorry," he said the words as though they were the very ones she had been waiting for. He was silent now, the sobs had ceased and he was waiting for her response.

Clair felt like a character in a silent movie, or rather, she corrected herself, the audience waiting for a cue card to tell them what the dialogue was. She cleared her throat. "Well. . . "

Paul was watching her with the look of a man who has done something unique and rather special and expects to be told so. Eighteen years, was all that Clair could think, eighteen years and I don't suppose he's ever said those words before.

His look of expectation hardened into need. "Can you forgive me?"

The sadness of his brown eyes was emphasized by the wet lashes. She saw for the first time the dark halfmoons of fatigue above his cheekbones, felt again something vaguely like her old affection for him.

"I don't know." She thought to ask him what she should forgive him for, but she knew he had a store of words, need, agony, accusations pent up and waiting for release if she turned the key by asking any question. She hoped to get away without carrying with her the weight of his guilt.

But he could not release her. "I told you not to have her come around here." It was not even an accusation, so weary and resigned was his voice.

Clair stood. She had expected this, been so prepared that she could not summon the anger she had felt sparking off her finger tips earlier in the day. Anger was an engagement and Clair wanted distance; she wanted to dip deep into the reservoir of herself and draw out what was smooth and cool and whole. She looked down at Paul whose head was bent forward again and he seemed to recede from her as she stood and watched him.

"I'm going to bed," she announced calmly.

"Yes," he nodded, "I'll be up in a minute.

It was then that Clair felt the panic begin to build, the smooth surface of calm begin to slip from her grasp and the ripples of hatred and anger begin to lap at the edges of her crumbling facade.

"Not tonight," she said, her voice tight across the chasm between them.

"All right." He looked up and smiled at her gently, resuming some of his superior stance and tone, allowing her this childish aberration, his magnanimity and maturity meant to make her seem small and selfish. "But soon, darling. I need you."

He rose from the chair, towered, it seemed, over her as he placed a hand on her shoulder, lightly kissed the top of her head. "Soon."

Clair turned and walked out of the room, panic nearly blinding her as she turned into the hall and tried to climb the stairs to the bedroom. She curled, fully clothed, on the top of the comforter, listening for Paul's movements downstairs. She heard nothing.

Clair lay on the bed listening and planning. Over and over she imagined the morning. In the morning, as soon as she heard Paul going out to the milking, she would go downstairs. When she heard the kitchen door slam and when she knew Paul was up in the barn, she would carry her packed boxes out to her small station wagon. She would put the boxes in her car — it wouldn't take more than ten minutes to carry them all out—and she would leave a note on the kitchen table for Paul. She would leave a note on the table when she walked out the door to get in her car and drive away. She would not look back.

# Chapter 14

Earlier, on the same night Clair had decided to leave, Anna drove slowly down the darkened road, her eyes adjusting imperfectly to the snowless spring landscape. Tonight the moon was out, but surrounded by a slight haze of moisture, it seemed to give no light. The car headlights shone a few yards ahead and then sank into the dirt road, muted, weighted by this heavy spring dark. She saw a light in the kitchen when she drove past Clair's, but as she came around the bend toward Elizabeth's house, Anna could see no light from the porch.

And when she drove up to the house, pulled into the yard by the kitchen, still she found no lights. She turned the car engine off and sat in the dark, waiting, listening, remembering.

"Come over after dinner tonight," Elizabeth had said, "I haven't seen you in weeks."

The words, exact, precise, were there in Anna's memory, recoverable. What she could not recover was the exact memory of what she felt in those weeks in February and March when she drove this road in anticipation of seeing Elizabeth, sitting close to her, touching her cheek and lips as she said goodnight on her way home.

"Come over after dinner tonight." The words were deceptively casual. Neither had just dropped by after their fight, Anna too caught in her own sense of humiliation and rejection, Elizabeth unwilling to feel the weight of Anna's need and desire. Anna had seen Tom's car parked in the drive and knew that he was home more and more frequently in these last weeks. As she realized what was happening, Anna's feelings began to turn from shame to anger. Elizabeth had used her: used her to repair her relationship with Tom, to escape from the involvement with Paul. Whatever physical desire she might still have for Elizabeth, Anna was also angry. So she had fixed a leisurely dinner, lingered over a cup of tea as she sat on the porch watching the final glow of a magenta evening sky. Finally she decided she would go, even though the anticipation of seeing Elizabeth was creating more anxiety than pleasure in her.

Through the open car window she could hear the spring night noises, loud, urgent, almost violent in their insistence. From the farm pond in the next field came the incessant rise and fall of peepers, a backdrop to the more abrupt chirp, croak and whistle of frogs and other night animals. For a moment she would hear all of the noise together in a near symphony of harmony and then it would slide into a meaningless cacophony. "Come over after dinner tonight." Elizabeth's car was here, but where was she? Anna opened the car door, climbed out and slammed it behind her. She stood in the barnyard in the dark, assessing, trying to remember what else Elizabeth might have said to explain this silence. One of the dogs emerged out of the barn, sniffed Anna's hand, wagged a brief tail, then melted back into the night. All seemed normal. It couldn't be later than eight thirty, even though she had lingered. She leaned back against her car in the warm night and waited.

She thought that Elizabeth might be waiting for her inside, sitting in the dark, enjoying a moment of quiet, wrapped in an envelope of solitide by the darkness as she waited for Anna. It would be like Elizabeth to turn off the lights, settle herself with a glass of wine, and wait. She would not doze, but remember – now Anna was creating for Elizabeth a memory she wanted her to possess – the feeling between them, the energy that came out of their intimacy. Those are not memories, a voice in Anna protested, those are only words. She will sit in the chair waiting for you and she will remember – this is how it works – she will remember how your hair fell across your face when you sat forward in your chair, remember how she wanted to reach over and brush it away, slide her hand along the softness of your face and flip the hair back over your collar. Or she will day dream and perhaps she will see you riding up the driveway in the snow storm that day, slouching in the saddle, your hat pulled down over your face as you guided the horse down the driveway through trackless snow. Perhaps that is how she will remember you.

Allowing this moment of nostalgia folded Anna's anger back beneath the surface and she felt then some of what had been, the poignancy of her own images of herself bringing the emotion out of the past. She could see herself in those moments, feel again some of the anticipation, remember what it was she had wanted on those nights when she had driven so eagerly up this driveway. She wished that Elizabeth would walk out of the house now, having heard Anna's car drive up. Anna wanted to hear the kitchen door open and shut. She peered through the dark shadows, willing Elizabeth's shape to form and walk toward her, Elizabeth's voice to call out a soft greeting, her firm hand to pull Anna toward her.

She waited for another moment, leaning against the car, buoyed by memory and nostalgia. Then the thread of that feeling led her to the kitchen door, her feet stepping surely across the dirt yard, directed by familiarity. Anna tapped lightly on the screen door and waited again.

"Elizabeth?" she called softly into the silence. "Hello?"

Now what? Anna stood staring into the kitchen through the unlocked screen door, unwilling to go forward, unable to retreat. She paused before this barrier which protected Elizabeth's privacy as she had paused so many times in months past before the less tangible barriers Elizabeth herself created, barriers of mood, of posture, of word, and, finally, of deed. When Elizabeth had slept with Paul, Anna felt, she placed an insurmountable barrier between them; that act separated them. And yet, why? Perhaps she was meant to see it as a challenge. Perhaps the failure was in her, that she had not been able or willing to push forward, when that was what would have secured the intimacy between them. Anna put her hand out toward the door and firmly pushed it open.

In the muted moonlight filtering through the room Anna could see the gleam of the white enamel hot water heater on the opposite wall. To her left was the dark doorway which led down the hall to the living room where she imagined Elizabeth was waiting for her. She waited, absorbing the odors of the kitchen: open compost by the sink waiting to be put out in the morning, dust, the musty smell of old wood paneling which circled the kitchen, waist-high. And the linoleum, always the cracked, deep-rose linoleum. She could feel the color under her feet as she stood on it, could remember how each night afer dinner Elizabeth had swept the crumbs from it with a broom, complaining that it protected more dirt than it prevented.

"Elizabeth," she called softly, reluctant to move forward without permission.

She could turn on the kitchen light, Anna thought, becoming practical for a moment. She could flick on this switch, next to her hand on the wall by the back door, and then she could see her way to the hall, turn on the hall light, and so to the living room. But she had entered the house without invitation, and felt compelled to finish her journey in darkness.

She edged forward toward the dark door, one hand lightly touching the wall beside her as a guide. Behind her she could hear, with preternaturally tuned ears, the drip, clink, clink of the water faucet in the kitchen sink. Ahead of her was a soft flap, flap which she though must be a curtain in the living room, blowing in an open window. Would Elizabeth be sitting by an open window on this evening? She did not know.

Anna paused before she turned the doorway into the living room. If Elizabeth was there, she knew by now that Anna was coming, had agreed by her silence to Anna's coming. Would she greet Anna with a joke? Or would the darkness give them a freedom they had not felt in the light? "Come back to me," the Rossetti lines started through her thoughts as she stood, one hand raised beside her, holding to the wall's firm surface. "Come back to me who wait and watch for you: Or come not yet, for it is over then." Her pulse racing, Anna turned into the living room.

It was empty. She could see that at a glance, as the moonlight came more strongly through the larger windows. She drew a deep breath. There were shadows, dark corners in the room, but she felt, as well as saw, that she was alone. Anna swallowed, disappointment clogging her throat.

The thread of feeling which had carried her into the house and down the hall was not broken. It led her around the periphery of the room, her hand resting briefly on a chair arm, on a book laid open, spine up, on the table between the two windows. She followed Elizabeth's presence through the room and then back toward the center, where she sat down in one of the two large chairs facing the cold dark hearth.

Anna sat in the moonlight, smelled the slightly acrid charcoal scent of yesterday's fire, felt the moist spring air on her skin. She knew, then, that she had never wanted anything the way she wanted Elizabeth to be waiting for her in that dark room, never *felt* so keenly as in that moment before she walked into this empty room. Not even as a child, in those open and covetous appetites of childhood, had she felt desire as she was feeling it now.

The pressure of that emotional hunger – thwarted – pushed harder and tighter inside Anna until it broke in anger. Like the shadow of a cloud crossing the moon, the darkness moved inside Anna. Where the hell is she? Her fists clenched and unclenched, the anger so much larger than the accidental missing of an appointment, of friends who have miscommunicated. She told me to come tonight, so where the hell is she? Anna's rage built step by step as she thought of herself, walking so carefully into the house, taking each step in the dark down to this living room where no one sat waiting for her. She was never there, a voice mocked Anna's expectation, not just tonight, she was never there for you, never there for you.

She sat rigid in the soft, worn chair, allowing her anger to possess her, but willing herself not to move, not to give in to this sudden and furious need to strike out, to throw something – herself, the chair, a lamp – against the wall or the high stone fireplace. The room around her became vivid in darkness. She could smell the life that was lived here, the scent of Elizabeth's presence and the children's was suddenly there for her, sharp against the stale ash in the fireplace. The glass base of a lamp in the far corner of the room pulsed and faded with light as the curtain blew a shadow over the moonlight and then withdrew. Anna felt, all at once, that Elizabeth might be upstairs asleep and the thread she had followed into the house and into this empty room seemed to leap toward the dark open staircase. Her anger focused, honed now to an object. She wanted to hurt Elizabeth.

She has forgotten you, the voice taunted again, why can't you just forget her? They're all asleep upstairs, maybe even Tom is there. You're makng a fool of yourself. Anna rose from her chair in a fury, but anger blinded her and she could not see to walk around the table toward the stairs. The thread was there but she could not seem to follow it. It led up the stairs to Elizabeth's bedroom and, for a moment, Anna felt herself accepting the challenge. She would go up the stairs, fling open the door to her bedroom and. . . and what? She heard the voice of her own sanity. So what the hell would you do? Rape her? No, the voice on the thread insisted, no. She's asleep, her barriers are down; she won't refuse me, this time she won't refuse me. But Anna was afraid, shocked at these feelings she had found within her. Shaken, she sat again, and the thread broke.

She sat still, dulled. The chair seemed unfamiliar to her body, the room a place of strange proportion and dimension. She felt as though parts of herself were scattered into new regions, lost in unfamiliar places, and she could not focus her thoughts, felt only the vague fear which had forced her back into her chair. Then one question surfaced, broke through the wide scattered darkness and caught the light: how could she have wanted to hurt Elizabeth? Finally, it was that of which she was afraid.

She could not remember another time, another incident in her life in which she had experienced a similar feeling. She searched her childhood, her young adulthood, for some scene, some argument which would place for her this desire to hurt Elizabeth. But she could find no parallel, no key through which she could understand what had just happened.

She had lost Elizabeth, that much was clear to Anna. The voice was right, Elizabeth had never been there for her. She had wanted Elizabeth, needed her, but never dared to ask for her. Anna dreamed that Elizabeth would say, "stay here with me," or "let me come with you." But how could Elizabeth have known what Anna wanted? Anna's expectations had come out of her own need. Elizabeth's needs were quite different. So why didn't she just feel grief at this loss? Why did she want to hurt Elizabeth? Anna remembered that when her mother had died she had felt loss. And, yes, she had felt anger, too, anger that she was left without her mother's care and comfort, even though as an adult she had left the immediacy of that need behind. But her mother was gone — irretrievably — and Elizabeth was still here wanting Anna's friendship, reminding her that what Anna had wanted was not possible to achieve, thwarted.

She had been thwarted in her work, too, Anna made that connection instantly. Why had she felt only grief when she had lost her job? Why hadn't she been angry? Why wasn't she angry now? In the moment of the question, Anna realized the falseness of the assumption. She was furious that she had lost her job, angry and hurt and furious to her very core, beyond expression and almost beyond allowing the knowledge of how angry she was. As she sat stiffly in her chair, Anna could feel the soft pad of anger's paws as it paced across her shoulders, up and down her spine. This anger brought danger, danger to herself, not to anyone else. For if she expressed this anger Anna was afriad that she could not go on working where she wanted to work. If she expressed this anger, she might never be able to get another job. The world told her this anger had to be contained, modified, redirected so that she could go on teaching. And, indeed, she had been so successful at disguising her feelings that she almost had not known they were there.

The meaning of this more hidden anger slowly began to dawn on Anna. She had known she could make mistakes, but she had not believed — in some very precious and protected part of herself — that she could be the "wrong" kind of person. "You're a good girl, Anna," her mother had told her, but now Anna felt she was not good enough, would never again find the easy acceptance of herself she was used to.

She had sat for hours at her desk one morning last week after her conversation with Lee, writing nothing at first, then turning to a new page. At the top of that blankness, she wrote the word lesbian. It was a revelation, Anna discovered, not a label — a revelation that allowed the words to pour out, to fill the emptiness she had struggled with for so long, as now she re-examined her own life and experience. She was not a new person, her experience was not different, nothing so simple as that. It was rather that key piece of the puzzle she was working on had been missing, and now with it in hand other moments, incidents, necessities, fell into place around it. Anna tried to remember the shock, the horror, she had felt the first time she heard that word — lesbian — spoken aloud, how she had rushed on past it, pretending not to notice. She no longer wanted to ignore it. Now the word evoked for her the intimacy of Elizabeth's living room, two women talking together in front of a fire as the cold gathered outside in the dark, surrounding, but unable to touch them. The word included Anna's shy pleasure at the recognition she felt when Lee asked, have you ever loved a woman? And it included also her pain and anger when that love was not returned. But it was not a word she would give up, for that would mean giving up some part of herself, allowing herself to be thwarted at some most basic, important level.

It seemed hard to her that she might have to choose between her need to do her own work, to love as she wished, and her need to be accepted, to be all right, to do what was expected of her. She had never had to make such a choice before. She always thought that what she wanted would be what the world would want from her. For a moment, Anna remembered Clair, her urgency to leave Paul and the way in which she had spent her whole life living with and accepting the thwarting of her most basic needs. Anna wondered why Clair had accepted the thwarting for so long, wondered what in Clair's past had shaped her acceptance, what in Anna's own past was now finally shaping her own rejection. For she would never again work or live or love as other people thought she ought. She supposed that meant she would have to learn to live with this anger balanced somewhere inside her, live with an anger that could be either friend or foe.

The room seemed to brighten as she looked around her. The formal old farmhouse parlour was familiar to her again as she sat resting, and prepared to leave. The lamps, the curved-leg end tables, were the same age and style as the furniture in her grandmother's parlour. Southwestern farmhouses were low, one story rambling buildings, not at all like this compact two story house built to hold the heat through long winters. But this furniture was why she had always felt at home in Elizabeth's living room. Anna had last sat in her grandmother's parlour when she flew home for her mother's funeral, left the coolness of a northeastern summer for the hot dry Oklahoma August. The air in that room was stuffy, aged. Especially in the summer, her grandmother kept the windows sealed, trying to keep out the insidious red dust travelling on every breath of air. Anna had felt then much as she did now, the early sense of loss, the anticipation of more emotion than she could touch in this first moment of grief. She felt like an amputee must feel, she told her grandmother, she had all of the sensations of feeling toward her mother, but she wasn't there. She held her grandmother's hand, looking down at the bent, loose-skinned hand with enlarged knuckles and raised veins running like soft dark water along the back.

"It's like I told your father," the old woman said to her then, "grief never leaves you where it finds you."

Anna sighed, stood to leave. She stepped toward the long dark hall, retracing her path in, letting her hand rest lightly on the wall, guiding her back toward the kitchen.

Out in the barnyard she was surprised by the light. The early evening haze had gone and the moonlight seemed to rest everywhere. She felt the newness of spring in the air, the anticipation of warmth and growth stayed with her as she walked to her car and drove out the familiar rutted path to the road. But against the freshness of this night and air she could still smell the dead ash from the cold hearth in the dark room she had left behind her.

# Chapter 15

"You could have let me know."

"I left a note on the front door."

"You know I haven't gone in the front door for months."

"I called you."

Anna and Elizabeth sat stiffly on the front porch in the orchard, the exuberance of spring swelling out around them, pushed back from the porch, Anna felt, by the cold distance between them. Anna could think of nothing to say.

"I'm sorry we missed you last night," Elizabeth had said tentatively as she walked toward the porch where Anna stood, tall, unbending, in front of her.

"We had to see the lawyer." Elizabeth nodded, urging Anna's recognition. Her lawyer's office was a three hour drive. She couldn't use a local lawyer, not one of Edward's friends. But Anna gave no sign.

"He was held up in court. It got so late. I did call, but I guess you'd already left."

Anna still was silent, but turned half toward her, eyes looking out to the trees. She did not want to see Elizabeth, did not want to look at her slightly browned warm skin, catch the glint of ice blue in her eyes.

Elizabeth took a breath, sighed deeply, and then said, "We're getting married as soon as the divorce is final, so we had to clear some things up."

Now Anna turned to look at her fully, eyebrows raised in silent surprise. Finally she had to speak. "You're marrying Tom?"

All of the reasons that Elizabeth might be doing this flashed through her mind as she asked the question: pregnancy first, then escape from Paul or Anna herself, Elizabeth's concern for her children.

"Why?" she asked.

Elizabeth shrugged. She felt judged, knew Anna did not approve of what she was doing and did not want to explain it to her. She searched briefly for an explanation Anna might approve of – custody of the children, security for the children – then she shrugged again.

"I'm pregnant," she said briefly, picking up a twig and scratching a hieroglyph in the hard mud by the porch step.

"Whose kid?" Anna's voice was harsh.

Did I deserve this? Elizabeth wondered, looking at Anna's frown, gauging her hostility. She shrugged. "Tom's. I'm nearly three months."

"You could get an abortion."

Elizabeth sighed again. "Let's walk," she said, gesturing toward the broad rows leading through the orchard and up the hill.

Anna hesitated and then agreed. She needed to stretch some of the ice out of her legs, her rigid body. She told herself again and again, it was a mistake. She just forgot. Anna realized how much anger at Elizabeth she still harbored, how badly she needed something to which she could attach this anger, lest it float around inside her, the hidden bulk of an iceberg ready to cause damage.

Elizabeth, too, knew that her absence last night had meant more to Anna than a mere oversight. She felt even more guilty, knowing that she had been relieved to be with Tom and the children in town, relieved not to have to see Anna yet. But here she was at eight o'clock in the morning. She had left Tom to cope with breakfast and she was standing in Anna's front yard to ask forgiveness. How silly. And yet, she cared. For every moment of reluctance and nervousness, Elizabeth had a moment of desire and concern. She could feel her emotional pulse swing wildly from one pole to the other – needing as she drove into the yard to be close to Anna, have her warmth and comfort, but feeling alienated, judged, as they stood to walk. She could only explain why she was marrying Tom when she felt Anna's distance.

"He's going to farm. We're going to build a life. The children need a father." The cliches sounded right to her from this distance. "I need help. I just can't manage alone any more."

This, at least, was true, Elizabeth felt, and true at the core of her, whichever mood she was in. She was exhausted, emotionally depleted, unable to summon her customary reserves. Oh yes, occasionally something seeped from her, like the old maples next to Anna's porch, but the real life of her seemed drained, and she did not know how to replenish it. She envied Anna her youth, the energy that allowed her to look forward to a new job, a new life. But she and Clair, Elizabeth thought, they were alike in this. They were at an age when a woman had to make do, take what life had given her and make the best of it. This she believed. And she wanted Anna to help her believe it, acquiesce in the inevitability of it before Anna left to try again, to try and create something new for herself.


Clair steered the car carefully around another spring pothole on the bumpy county road she was following south. Signs for the Taconic Parkway were beginning to appear. The Taconic meant the city. When she reached the Taconic, it would be as though she were almost there.

Full sunrise had greeted her as she pulled out of the driveway of the farm and turned down the road. She did not look back, not even in the rearview mirror, afraid she would see Paul, surprised away from milking by the sound of her car engine, see him looking out the wide barn doors toward her. If she did not see him, she felt perhaps he would not have heard her. Perhaps the noise of the milking machine would have covered the noise of her departure. And so she did not look back. She cherished her anger. She carried no nostalgia with her.

Once on the country road the sun was so low and strong on the southeastern horizon that she had to lower the visor on the windshield. Exhaustion from the sleepless night began to seep out of her body as she drove. With each mile her breathing relaxed, the pounding in the head, the throb of the artery on the side of her neck subsided. The words of the note she left on the kitchen table for Paul to find when he came back from milking played through her thoughts, as they had all night while she composed—not an explanation, not a reason, but the terms of this separation. *I have taken a set of checks. I know you can afford this.* How did she know? She had no knowledge, and yet she knew Anna was right. She knew there was money, investments, other accounts. There was always money when Paul needed it. *On the first of each month I will draw $600.00 from our account.* She did not know how much to say she would take. All night she worried about the money, worried whether she could get a job, support herself, pay for rent, food.

She was a child going into an adult world. I'm forty three and I don't know how much it costs for one person to live for one month, she thought angrily.

She did not tell Paul where she was going, what she would do. She did not know. And the children. She willed herself not to think of the children just now. That was for later. *Tell the children I will write to each of them.* No pleas for them to understand, she knew they could not. No protestations of love they would not believe. *Tell them I will write to each of them.* It was all she could say.

So, Anna thought to herself, this will make it harder for Clair to leave. She wondered if things would go back to normal with Paul and Clair. But for Elizabeth. This seemed so drastic, so complete, as though Elizabeth were finished, somehow.

"Can't you get some help without binding yourself to Tom?" she asked. "When I first met you what you wanted most was to be independent. I know it's hard, with the children and all. But there must be a way. . ." Her voice trailed off in her memory of the way she had wanted Elizabeth to find help.

They walked toward the rising sun through ankle high, dew wet, spring green grass which bent flat under their steps. Glancing back Anna could see their footprints in the grass as distinctly as if they had been walking on a sandy beach. She felt, after her experience in the dark last night, that her skin was soft and new like the grass, and each word left a soft dent, a tangible mark of its passing.

"So why not an abortion?" she asked finally, breaking the human silence, breaking into the chorus of birds and insects rising on all sides of them through the fresh air.

Why not an abortion? Elizabeth sighed. It was the obvious question, the one she was least able to answer.

"I guess I just don't have the strength." She half laughed at Anna's raised inquiring eyebrow. "I know. It seems like having another kid would take more strength, especially like this. . ." Anna nodded. "But an abortion. I would have had to do that by myself." Her voice was introspective now, not addressing Anna. "I mean, I wouldn't have told Tom I was even pregnant with his kid if I were getting an abortion. I don't think I could have asked him to support me in that." She paused again. "He would have, though." She sounded surprised by the memory. "It was the first thing he said," she told Anna. "We'll get an abortion."

"Why did that surprise you? It's what I would have expected him to say. I'm surprised he wants to get married."

Elizabeth was still in her own reverie — unaware of Anna as a woman who loved her, who was disappointed in her — as she searched for her own necessities.

"He would have known," she said, pausing. "He would have known that I didn't mean to stay, that I was only using him." The words came very slowly. "And I would have known that I couldn't have gotten away from Edward on my own. That it's too much. The children. I used Tom to get away." She had almost completely forgotten that Anna was walking with her. Did this mean she wouldn't be able to leave Tom either? And finally, the realization. If I'd had the abortion I would have been free. I would have been on my own. She drew a deep breath and looked up, seeing Anna. She could not say these things out loud.

They stood for a moment on the top of the hill. As Anna looked at the orchard stretching out before her, each tree pruned and shaped so precisely to bear fruit, they seemed — in this moment before the buds blossomed into flowers which would hide the bare twisted limbs — almost grotesque, not trees at all, but a surrealistic mockery of trees. She could not remember ever perceiving them so before.

"You'll find a man." Elizabeth was consoling her.

"No."

"How do you know? How can you predict?"

"I know." Anna was stubbornly insistent. "I know I want a woman. I want to be with a woman."

"We can't all live the way you do." Elizabeth's voice now sounded harsh, even to herself. She tempered her tone. "I just mean that life doesn't give us all the same choices. I have to make the best of what I've got. That's all I can do."

Anna heard the plea in Elizabeth's last words and nodded, giving up something in the gesture. She wondered where it went, all that energy of self that some women have to tamp down, protect, nourish in secret. Did it last or slip away? Or did it explode like gunpowder, pushed down into the cartridge, packed tight and waiting for a spark?

She nodded again. "I'll ride Rose over to Pam next weekend, if that seems O.K."

Elizabeth laughed, relieved they were finished talking. "O.K.? This is the event of a lifetime. I won't tell Pam yet or she won't sleep all week. She's already changed the hay in the stall twice and there's no horse in it yet."

Anna was smiling. "I was like that. I remember my first horse. There's nothing like it."


Paul walked down to the house from the barn. Milking had taken longer this morning, the herd was producing more heavily and spring seemed to make them less docile, less manageable. Cows who went quietly every day to their own stanchions and waited for the milker to be suctioned onto their nipples, now forgot where they belonged, ignored the absolute order with which they always filed into the barn, bucked, pushed, lowed, and then kicked as he wiped their nipples with disinfectant. Irritation didn't help. Paul had to keep calm, so that he could quiet and soothe the herd or the milking would never get done. This morning he didn't mind. He felt as though he had a large store of patience. He had been patient with Clair last night, and his patience grew and expanded in anticipation of his reward. He reflected, as he walked down toward breakfast, that this might not have been a bad thing, what happened between him and Clair. They would talk now. She would come around. He felt warm and forgiving without realizing how easy he found it to forgive himself, expecting that Clair would be feeling this morning the way he needed her to feel.

Somewhere between the old foundation and the path leading over to the plowed garden Paul began to feel unsettled, slightly on edge. As he came to the back door, the house was silent. Clair was apparently not up yet, nor the children. He was annoyed, wanting his coffee ready. He leaned over to pull off his boots and stopped suddenly, seeing that Clair's car was not parked next to the truck in the driveway. Her car was gone. He looked around again as though it might be parked anywhere else. It was gone. He pulled off his other boot and went into the kitchen. Clair turned onto the Taconic as Paul walked into the kitchen. She could not have known, but did know, the exact moment when he reached for her letter, left in the center of the table. She settled down into the worn upholstery of the car seat and smiled at the sign announcing New York City – 110. She felt like a child at Christmas now, excited

146

and not at all afraid. It's like a present to myself. Her pleasure was real and grew warm and radiant as she considered it, layering over the fear she had carried with her that Paul might try to stop her, even now. Last night, lying awake on their bed, listening for Paul's step on the stair, she had been afraid that he would say she was mad again, call the police or the hospital when he read her letter, send someone after her to stop her, haul her back, tell her she could not do what she wanted to do. And so she made her letter very calm, rational, business-like in its tone and substance. She would give him no excuse to say she was not in complete control. She wondered dispassionately whether he would be angry when he read the letter, or whether he would cry again, as he had last night.

Elizabeth drove out of Anna's driveway relieved, feeling that something had been resolved, although she could not say what it was. As she drove toward home she glanced up toward Clair and Paul's and decided to stop in for a cup of coffee with Clair. She wanted to talk to Clair. She supposed Paul had told her the news by now. But talking with Anna had left her unsettled. As soon as she thought of Clair, she realized she could say things to her she couldn't say to Anna. She drove in, parked next to the truck and walked up to the back porch.

She did not smell coffee brewing and, as she reached up tentatively to knock, she saw Paul seated at the kitchen table, his head fallen forward, his whole body slumped, propped on the table.

"Paul?" He did not answer or look up. Oh, shit, Elizabeth thought instantly. I shouldn't have come. I don't need any more trouble, not now, not right now. But she could not walk away. She pushed open the kitchen door and went in to Paul.

He was breathing, she saw at once, so that wasn't it. She stood next to him and reached her hand out to his shoulder. As she did so, she saw the letter on the table written in Clair's hand and, without reading it, she knew. Clair was gone. No other possibility even presented itself to Elizabeth, not suicide or an accident or illness, she knew at once that Clair had left. She was stunned, nearly breathless, standing absolutely still next to Paul, one hand on his shoulder, her eyes riveted on the letter lying in the middle of the kitchen table, carelessly flung, the two pages open, revealing. She stared and stared at the letter written in

Clair's hand and from somewhere very distant, she heard Paul begin to speak.

". . . just getting back just getting to be ourselves again, talk again. I don't understand. Why now?" His voice was low and hoarse with grief and tears, yet from where Elizabeth heard him, it seemed almost like a childish whine. "Why now when things were getting back to normal?" God, she thought, the man is an idiot. She didn't want you back. Why should she? And then Elizabeth's clarity was shaken, her visceral understanding of what Clair had done and why, was overwhelmed by her own anger. Clair had left, she had left Paul and she had left the children, for Elizabeth could hear the girl's voices and footsteps upstairs as they started to rouse themselves. And all of a sudden she was furious at Clair. How could she have left the children, how could she?

She did not realize she was speaking outloud until Paul began to answer her. "I don't know, she just did it, she didn't even leave them a message or an explanation," he said bitterly, waving his hand toward the letter, a silent accuser lying in the center of the table.

Elizabeth was shaking her head, pacing heatedly the length of the kitchen and back. "She must be mad. How could she leave the children, you just don't leave the children, she's nuts." There was no time to examine this response, so suddenly did Elizabeth find herself overwhelmed by her rage at Clair's behavior. She could not pause, find her balance, realize the source of her anger.

As she paced she began to feel Paul watching her closely, listening to her words. "You're right," he said, standing abruptly. The whine was gone fom his voice and this new tone made her pay attention. "You're right. This isn't normal. She must be having another breakdown. We'll have to bring her back." He turned toward Elizabeth and held out his hands, appealing, "You'll help me, won't you?"

"What?" She had heard him but did not know what he meant.

"Bring her back. You'll help me bring her back, won't you? She can't be well or she wouldn't have done this." He was beginning to convince himself now.

"I don't understand." Elizabeth was confused. "Do you know where she is? Can you call her and ask her to come home?"

"No. I don't know where she is. That's why I think she's not quite right. I mean she didn't even say where she was going." He picked up the letter and waved it at Elizabeth. His voice was very firm now. "I'll call the police. And the hospital. They'll have to find her. She can't be well." He didn't feel quite comfortable with the way Elizabeth was looking at him, but moved toward the phone.

"Don't you dare." Her voice was sharp. What was he doing? This wasn't what she had meant at all. He knew that. Why was he doing this? Paul hesitated, then moved toward the phone again.

"I mean it, Paul. I'll stop you. You know there's nothing wrong with Clair. She's just left you. That doesn't make her mad. You know that is not what I meant." She made herself sound very authoratative, drew herself up to full height and crossed her arms firmly over her chest. "I'll stop you." She had no idea how she would do this if he went on. He paused and looked at her, not sure now.

"How do you think it would look? They'd be laughing themselves silly. Hysterical man calls because wife left him." It was cruel, she knew, but she had to make sure he wouldn't hurt Clair. He stood, looking at her, the worried, slumped look coming back as she watched him. Elizabeth could hear the children coming down the stairs now. She turned to leave, taking with her this bundle of strange responses.

How will it end? She wondered as she drove out of the driveway again. What will become of Clair? And of Paul? She paused at the end of the drive as if she did not know which way she meant to turn. Where had she been going? Home, of course, to tell Tom what was happening. Home. She turned right onto the road. It was the only way she could go.


Anna wandered lonely through her little house after Elizabeth had left, another cup of coffee in her hand, contemplating each group of objects she would have to pack in the next week. She didn't have much. Not even a bed or chair. All she owned were her personal belongings, books, a few prints, some plants and vases, dishes, her clothes. Not a lot, but she wished it were more or less. This "in between" was too much to load into Betsy and fade into the sunset with and too little to hire a mover to come in for. She felt ready to leave, but didn't want to have to do the work of leaving. Too bad she couldn't put a sandwich in her saddlebag and ride away on Rose, leaving all of this. None of it seemed particularly connected to her now. These books were not the books she needed to read again, that Picasso clown print was not something she wanted to look at any more.

As she sat staring at the bookshelf, she heard a truck rattle into her driveway. It must be Chip with the U-Haul trailer. She shook herself out of lethargy and went back out into the sun.

"Too nice to be inside today," he looked up briefly from disengaging the trailer hitch. His voice felt brusque to Anna.

"Yeah." Suddenly she didn't know what else to say.

After a moment he freed the trailer and settled the hitch on the ground. "Well, it's yours for two weeks. They expect it in Portland two weeks from today. Think you can make it?" He was looking at the ground, then gazing around at the trees, his eyes above or below Anna's. "You all packed?" he asked, nodding toward the house.

"Packed? Are you kidding? I was just standing in there wondering if I couldn't leave it all and ride away on Rose." Anna half laughed, shrugged.

"Oh. Well, I thought you were so anxious to get out of here." He was looking at his feet now and Anna began to understand.

"It's real hard to leave," she admitted. "But waiting till August won't make it any easier." He nodded and they stood in silence for a moment. Then Chip swung the trailer hitch around and pushed it to one side so he could back his truck out.

"Well, I did get used to you living here. Seem strange to have the place shut up again." His eyes rested contemplatively on the little house.

"I'll miss you, too, Chip," Anna said, refusing to be indirect any longer. She sighed. What to say? "Knowing you has been real important to me. And I'll miss our talks. And the orchard." She turned away from him and stood looking out at the trees. "Anyway," she turned back to him, smiling, forcing him to meet her eyes, "I've got a whole week left and I intend to spend a lot of it walking and riding out here in the orchard. So we don't have to say goodbye yet, O.K.?"

"Sure." He ran a nervous hand through his hair, turned to leave. "You'll be fine," he nodded at Anna's old car. "I've tuned Betsy within an inch of her life, so you'll make it across the mountains. Just don't put all the books on one side when you load it."

"Promise," Anna laughed.

# *May*

It was the last sunset of her last day in the orchard. Rain had threatened all afternoon, but not fallen. Now the horizon reddened as the sun sank under the clouds, but rested above the mountains. Anna walked out to the barn and bridled Rose. She had already packed the saddle and tack. She led the horse over to the porch and mounted bareback from the steps.

I've said all the goodbyes except this one, Anna thought, as she turned Rose's head toward the sunset and climbed the hill westward.

The trees had been in blossom for three days, the fresh sweet scent filling the air, wafting into the house as Anna packed, sorted, filled boxes and carried them to the trailer. She felt physically, exquisitely attached to this landscape, and did not know yet what it would mean to leave it. The orchard seemed determined to make this farewell the most difficult. Anna could not remember when it had been more beautiful. Rose waded fetlock deep through the unmown green grass. Around her the blossoms, pink and white, hung heavily on each branch and twig. The hum of bees filled the air and the lighter chirrup of the birds, satisfied, at the end of a day, hung on the breeze.

Anna rode slowly, her thighs snug against Rose's smooth warm back. She wanted something from the orchard tonight, something she could take away with her in the morning when she drove down this dirt road for the last time. As she rode, she felt some of the frustration, the anger and bitterness of the last months, begin to lift from her shoulders. She came to the top of the hill. The sun highlighted the clouds that had hung in the sky all afternoon, heavy with unshed rain, and Anna was weighted, heavy again for a moment with her own unshed tears.

She wanted to be a new person in her new place. Then she smiled. She was a new person, sort of, and a new place meant she could be seen newly, freshly. She was going alone, a woman alone.

The sky was slate grey when she pulled the horse's head up from where she had been grazing and started down the hill.

Photo: Clara Cohan

**JUDITH McDANIEL** is a feminist writer, publisher, teacher, co-founder and former editor and publisher of Spinsters, Ink, a radical feminist publishing house. She has taught literature and creative writing at universities and prisons. She is chair of the Literature Panel of the N.Y. State Council on the Arts and former chair of the Skidmore College Women's Studies Program and the State of Vermont Task Force on Rape Crisis. Her articles, interviews, fiction and reviews appear in feminist and scholarly journals. A collection of her poetry, *November Woman*, was published in 1983.

Spinsters, Ink is a women's independent publishing company that survives despite financial and cultural obstacles. Our commitment is to publishing works of literature and non-fiction that are beyond the scope of mainstream commercial publishers. We emphasize work by feminists and lesbians.

Your support through buying our books or making donations will enable us to continue to bring out new books—to publish between the cracks of what can be imagined and what will be accepted.

For a complete list of our titles, please write to us.

Spinsters, Ink
803 De Haro St.
San Francisco, CA 94107